Paltadi

By

MOG P.

INDIA · SINGAPORE · MALAYSIA

Disclaimer

This book is a work of fiction. All characters depicted in the book are fictional. Any resemblance to any person/persons deceased or alive is purely coincidental.

Dedicated to my children,
Evan and Faith

Contents

Preface

Paltadi

I stand on my side of the river and intently gaze upon the other side. I wonder what it's like there. What are the people like? Are they happier than I am? Or are they not? This is the definition of *Paltadi*. It means the other side. The fact of the matter might be that the people we wonder about are not very different from us. They all experience the same range of emotions that we do and let these shape their lives for better or for worse.

This book is a collection of stories about people and relationships. We all love stories. They have the power to touch our lives and stay with us forever. Stories in the written form are so much more profound than what we watch on screen. It's because they make us visualize and stretch our imaginations, and may be even teach us a thing or two. Therefore, writing is one of my great loves. The other, is my home state of Goa, India. And so, I decided to marry the two. Interwoven through the fabric of all these stories is the essence of Goa. Through them, I wish to preserve my memories of the Goan way of life as I have known it.

There are thousands of people who share my love for Goa. This tiny haven is under threat from powerful forces like greed and apathy. This book is a small attempt to remember the good things and to give back as much as I can, to this my home.

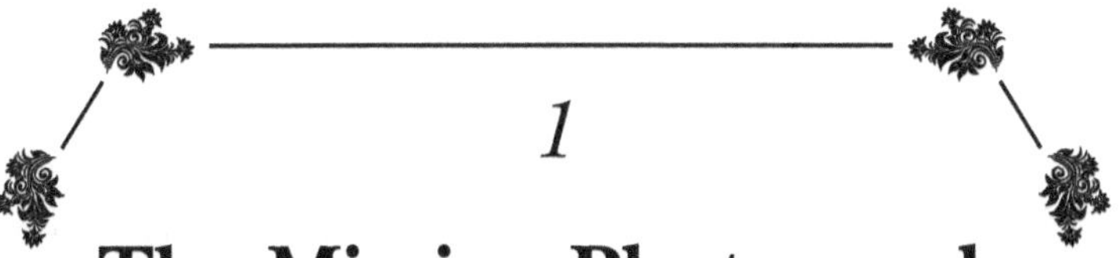

1

The Missing Photograph

The chill in the night air sent a shiver right through Chloe. She wrapped the shawl around her shoulders tighter and snuggled into its soft comfort as she watched the stars out of the tall open window. The high ceilings of the old house embraced the cold air that floated in. The last of the mourners had left hours ago. Chloe couldn't help but feel all alone. The death of her maternal grandmother meant that the last member of her immediate family was gone.

It was the second of November, All Souls day. What a coincidence that her Avozinha had died on All Saints Day, to be buried on All Souls Day. Or perhaps Chloe thought, it was the way her fastidious Avozinha had chosen to go on the most appropriate of all days. 'I wouldn't put it past her', Chloe smiled to herself. She had never known anyone as formidable as her Avozinha. She had raised Chloe ever since both her parents had perished in a road accident when Chloe had been but ten years old.

In her prime, Avozinha had been considered to be an heiress – the only child and daughter of affluent parents. She had been endowed with their opulent ancestral mansion and fortune. Avozinha had in turn produced a single child, a daughter, Chloe's mother. And Chloe's mother had in turn borne only Chloe. Chloe was therefore the third generation of only children who were daughters.

Chloe's father had been an orphan. Her mama had caused quite the scandal when she'd decided to marry him, 'a nobody' against her distinguished mothers' wishes. Chloe had been told that Avozinha had been livid and had cut off the young couple completely. However, some years later, a chance encounter with the then-three-year-old Chloe had thawed her steel heart. She had fallen in love with the granddaughter who bore the same distinct grey-green eyes as her. For Chloe's sake, Avozinha had reconciled with her estranged daughter and son-in-law.

Chloe who had been a beautiful child had indeed grown up into a gorgeous young woman. Avozinha had always been proud of her lovely granddaughter. She had raised Chloe to be a proper young lady. When she turned eighteen, Chloe asked Avozinha for permission to enter the Miss India contest. She wanted to become a model. It was not surprising that Avozinha was very reluctant. But Chloe had begged and pleaded and she had finally conceded. The fact was that Avozinha had been more concerned about losing Chloe rather than how appropriate her choice of career was. Her worst fears were realized. The contest launched Chloe's modelling career, which in turn kept Chloe away from home and Avozinha for years on end. Unknown to Chloe, Avozinha had spent her last years pining for her precious grandchild whose visits were rare and far between.

At twenty-seven years of age, Chloe was still at the top of her profession. But on the dark night of her Avozinha's funeral day, she couldn't help but come to the crushing realization that she was indeed all alone. She had no real friends in her profession and had been careless about maintaining relationships with friends from her childhood whom she had left behind almost a decade ago. She was certain that by now the rifts were too deep to mend. She had many admirers, but not one she could trust enough to call her own.

The cold night air sent another shiver down her spine reminding her that it was time to get off her perch on the window. She pulled it shut. She wrapped her shawl tightly around herself and wandered through the large looming house that was now hers. The old house was meticulously maintained. This included the two wide halls with their ancient chandeliers that still sparkled in the light, the ornately carved furniture, the antique pieces of delicate china, and the intricate paintings of landscapes that hung on the walls. It all bore witness to Avozinha's pride ad care. She vowed that she would not let even a single inch of the sacred space fall into disrepair. She would care for this legacy with every available ounce of herself. The thought made her feel even more alone.

Great artistic talent had always run in the family. Avonzinha painted intricate landscapes and natural scenes that hung on almost all of the walls throughout the house. Chloe's mother had ventured into painting faces and the human form. Her work was a little more abstract and a few of her pieces were hung in the suite of dual rooms which had been occupied by Chloe's parents. Chloe had been a talented artist herself. She was an even more talented photographer. But she had never felt the urge to pursue it. Her passion as a youngster had been modelling. Being beautiful had narrowed her outlook on life, she sadly thought to herself. She had decided to take an extended break from work. Her agency was not happy about her hiatus, but she didn't really care. She felt the need to become grounded again, to be able to reconnect with her roots even though it was far too late by all accounts.

Chloe could not sleep. Her mind was constantly filled with memories from childhood, of all the people that she had lost forever – her parents and her Avozinha. She tossed and turned, pulling up the sheets close to her, trying to cocoon and comfort herself in vain. Even through the happiest of childhood memories, the ghost of profound loss and loneliness haunted her, forcing her to acknowledge that she was now effectively orphaned.

When she could take it no more, she tossed the sheets aside and got out of bed. An invisible hand led her to the large ornate trunk that stood on long curved limbs outside her Avozinha's room. It was filled with photo albums, lovingly wrapped in silk, and sprinkled with mothballs. These contained photographs and memories that went back several decades. She opened the trunk and carried armfuls of the albums onto her grandmother's bed. She arranged them in the same order as she'd removed them. Right at the top, were fairly recent albums with pictures from her modelling career – pictures that she had sent her Avozinha. These had all been painstakingly arranged in order of chronology.

She set the one aside and moved to the next which contained pictures of her childhood including pictures taken with her parents mainly at birthday parties and family gatherings. She couldn't help the tears that flowed and continued leafing through the heavy pages. She found a rare photograph of her parents on their wedding day – her mother in a simple white dress smiling up serenely at her husband, devoid of all the finery that must have been originally planned for her. There was only one more copy of this picture which was framed and stood in her late parents' room.

She moved slowly from album to album – her mother as a child, her grandmother as a handsome young woman at the helm of a black ambassador car. Avozinha had been the first to own and drive a car in the village, let alone be the first woman driver. 'How unheard of it must have been in her day! What attention it must have drawn, undesirable or otherwise! ', Chloe thought to herself in awe. She smiled as she imagined the defiant glare that her Avozinha must have surely used to shoot down any of her detractors. Chloe had never known anyone as strong as her.

Right at the bottom of the old trunk, there laid a parcel carefully wrapped in faded blue velvet. Chloe was careful as she unwrapped what was the last photo album in the collection. Like all of the older albums, this one was made of thick paper with leaves of thick black paper separated by yellowing sheets of thin tissue-like paper. Black and white photographs were stuck on the black pages with an adhesive applied only at the four corners of each picture. The pictures all had white borders which were trimmed into holly leaf-like patterns. Chloe carefully opened the precious album and lifted the crinkly tissue from over the first photograph. It was a picture of a handsome middle-aged couple.

The gentleman was in a formal suit, vest and tie. His dark hair was slicked back and his dark moustache was smartly upturned at its corners. The lady wore a high-collared, long-sleeved gown with a cameo broach at her neck, her hair pulled back into a severe bun at the top of her head. They could only be her great-grandparents. Avozinha's father had been a prominent physician, well respected in the ranks of the then Portuguese administration. The little road that led to their mansion still bore his name, 'Voiz Francisco' road. Avozinha had adored her father. She had inherited her striking grey-green eyes from him. In those eyes, he could do no wrong. He had insisted on educating her well and had possibly made every important decision in her life including whom she would marry. Yet he had managed to empower her, never letting her forget that she was his heir and successor in every way.

Avozinha had often spoken about her father, wistfully and fondly. It was obvious that he had been the biggest influence on her life. Chloe reminisced about these conversations as she stared at the picture of the stately couple who looked back at her solemnly. She turned the page and found a picture of a little girl with a head full of ringlets and vivid eyes. The child was no more than nine or ten years old. She carried a small bunch of flowers, and the scene was staged in an old-fashioned photo studio. She smiled at the child who would grow up to be her Avozinha.

The picture was affixed on the right-hand side of the back page. There were tell-tale signs of a blank space on the left-hand side of the page. It appeared that another picture of the same dimensions had been removed. This was evident by the traces of adhesive which must have been applied to its four corners. The missing photograph had also left behind a dark serrated rectangle of black that stood out against its slightly faded surroundings.

Chloe gently traced the sides of the rectangle in contemplation of who the picture might have captured. The right-hand side of the next page contained another picture of her Avozinha, slightly older than the child on the previous page. The left side again bore signs of the gaping black rectangle that had probably contained another picture. The album bore four more pages that followed the same pattern. In every new picture, her Avozinha was slightly older than the last. On the last of the four pages which were arranged in this manner, the photograph revealed a lovely young woman.

The final page of the album broke from the pattern and contained a single photograph at its centre – that of her Avozinha in a flowing gown clasping a bouquet of small flowers and staring dreamily into space with her striking eyes. This was probably the picture that was used to accompany proposals of marriage back in the day. Chloe admired the beauty that her grandmother had once been. She had indeed been more striking than Chloe. She smiled at the thought of her grandmother being model material.

The sojourn through photographs of family generations seemed to have an uplifting effect on Chloe's drooping spirits. This prompted her to get comfortable and fall into sound sleep on her Avozinha's wide and soft bed, with the stacks of photo albums spread all around her.

The sky was flooded with light when Chloe woke up the next morning to the sound of the doorbell being used in combination with the metal knocker. She dragged herself out of bed and staggered towards the front door. It was Angela, Avozinha's long-time and trusted employee who came in six days a week to clean the house and do some light cooking. The previous day, Chloe had requested Angela to keep coming in as she usually did, since she had not much of an idea of what her plans for the future would be. She supposed that she would have to hire a caretaker if she went back to Mumbai, where her modelling career was. She had not really had the time to think things through, but she was happy to have Angela around the house. She greeted Angela like the old friend she was and let her in. Angela quickly set about her all too familiar chores. This familiar sight in itself brought Chloe a big sense of comfort.

Chloe went into the kitchen after freshening up and changing into a comfortable set of clothes. She made herself a cup of coffee, sliced open a stale poie and toasted it on a tawa. Avozinha did not have a toaster and Chloe had never gotten around to buying her one even though she'd intended to. She felt a fresh stab of guilt for having been so neglectful. How her Avozinha had managed all alone in this large lonesome house was beyond her.

Besides Angela, Avozinha had a couple of other hired hands who did the heavy lifting. There was Pauline who came to spend nights with her and a neglectful granddaughter who barely visited. Chloe could feel the now familiar acute sense of loss and regret rising through her again. It wouldn't do! She had too much to take care of, so she tried her best to suppress it. But it floated all around her like steam rising from a geyser that went down to her core. She discovered fresh tears and decided to silently accept them along with her coffee and toast.

She walked back to Avozinha's room and pulled out the old album wrapped in blue velvet. She gazed at the pictures of Avozinha's childhood and youth fondly, all the while conscious of the stark mysterious space next to it. She was intrigued by the missing photographs. Then on the first of the pages with the missing photograph, she noticed a tiny scrawl in pencil. It was rendered apparent only because of the natural sunlight that streamed into the room. Chloe was quick to retrieve a magnifying glass from her old room. She was able to make out the words *'Emma e Esmeralda, mieu angels'* in a small cursive hand. Avozinha was Esmeralda, and Emma? She wondered. Did Avozinha have a sister? If so, then why had she never once mentioned her? Perhaps she had died tragically young, and the memories had been simply too painful to handle. But why had all the pictures been removed? It was as though someone wanted all trace of her gone.

Why? Chloe was infinitely intrigued. There was no letting go of this now. She was struck by a sudden realization and sprang out of her chair. She went into the halls and minutely looked at all of Avozinha's paintings. In almost every one of her paintings of landscapes, Avozinha had depicted two small figures walking, sitting, or playing together. They were so skillfully camouflaged or faded away in the background, that no one would notice them without careful observation.

Chloe was now even more convinced that Emma had been Avozinha's sister or at least a very close relative. She wondered what manner of tragedy had befallen the family that they had chosen to forget Emma. She needed to find out. Her mind was resolute. She would search every room of the old house from the rafters to the floor if she had to. It was unfortunate that Avozinha never kept a journal. It would have been far easier if she had. But there had to be another way.

After gulping down the rest of her coffee, Chloe locked herself in Avozinha's room and began a long, meticulous search. She emptied Avozinha's wardrobe, dresser and other drawers. She went through the contents thoroughly. Thankfully her conscientious

Avozinha had been diligent with her records and belongings. Chloe was careful to replace everything just as she had found it. She worked from lunchtime until evening, at which point in time she realized that she was tired and famished. When she left Avozinha's room, daylight was fading. Angela had left and the house would soon be in utter darkness.

Chloe quickly walked through the house turning on lights in the common areas and shutting windows before the mosquitos came in. Then, she went to the kitchen and found a pot of reheated stew on the stove. There were fresh loaves of pao from the baker who must have made his evening rounds. She thanked Angela silently and then ate a hearty meal. She normally followed a carefully planned regimen of food and exercise. But she had rudely abandoned all of that as soon as she had been informed about Avozinha's passing. She let out a long sigh as soon as she had wiped clean the last smidge of gravy with her last crumb of pao and swallowed it. Her efforts in Avozinha's room had yielded nothing. There was no trace of Emma, not even a mention of the name anywhere. It would take her at least a week if not more to look through the rest of the house. It was not a matter of having the time or putting in the effort. It was just that Avozinha's room had been the likeliest of places where she could find something. Yet, there was nothing to be found.

She heard the distant toll of the church bell and knew that it meant that it was 7.00 PM and time for the Angelus. Avozinha always lit candles at the altar at this hour and recited the Angelus. Chloe would do the same. The ornate altar was over six feet in height with pointed arches and twisted spires. It looked like a miniature cathedral. The dark wood housed a chamber framed in glass and painted a pale blue inside. It housed a large crucifix with a statue in the image of Christ and was flanked on either side by statues of Mother Mary and Saint Joseph. A bunch of handmade red velvet roses had faded into mauve after years inside the glass chamber.

Chloe lit the candles and began reciting the Angelus by heart. It had been almost a decade since she had recited the prayer, yet it simply poured out of her unhindered. It had been ingrained in her mind since childhood, she would never forget it. She prayed for her grandmother, and she prayed for strength and guidance. As she drew close to the altar again, she noticed a silver glint from its inner sanctum. It was the silver rosary that her Avozinha had gifted her on her first holy communion. She thought that she had lost it years ago. But there it was! She carefully opened the framed glass door of the chamber to take it out. She noticed yellowing paper peeking from under the heavy statue of Mother Mary. She carefully extracted both items and found that the yellowing paper was an old unaddressed heavy envelope. She took it to the light and opened it. It produced a few old black-and-white photographs of a girl. Chloe gasped. She had found the missing photographs! She had found Emma!

Upon studying the photographs, Chloe discovered that the back of every photo bore Emma's name, age, and the date on which the photograph had been taken.

These were written in the same hand as the pencil inscription on the first of the pages. Chloe removed Avozinha's photographs from the album and found the same inscriptions on the back. There was a resemblance between the two girls, especially in the eyes. They both had the same striking eyes as Avozinha's father. Chloe was now certain that the two were sisters. Chloe had further deduced that the sisters were two years apart. Emma was the older of the two. But Chloe could not fathom why Avozinha had never spoken about her sister. Had her untimely death been too painful to recount? Or was it something else altogether that has estranged Emma from her family? Chloe would find out soon.

It was only a few hours later, the next morning to be precise, when Chloe visited the church to finalise a few arrangements regarding her Avozinha's grave. She walked into the church office to find Padvigar immersed in paperwork. The office was rather antiquated with several glass-encased bookcases containing thick registers each labelled neatly on their spines with the year. These were all records of baptisms, marriages, and deaths in the parish, going back many years. Chloe had a sudden moment of enlightenment. She could find several answers in this place. She patiently waited for Padvigar to spare her some time and then explained her predicament to him. She pleaded to be allowed access to records at the earliest. The kindly old man agreed to help her, especially for the sake of her late grandmother, who he held in high esteem. Chloe would need to fill in some paperwork and the office assistant would help her in her quest. Chloe was delighted. It was the first time since hearing of Avozinha's death that she'd felt this positive, and most importantly, hopeful.

She visited the church office the next morning as per Padvigar's instructions. She had done her homework the previous day and figured out the year in which Emma was born. She was relieved that the birth register for that year was still in the same office and not in some musty archive. She carefully thumbed her way through the old pages of the register, its paper soft and feathery to the touch.

Emma Maria Eutemia Antoinette Sousa had been born in the summer and baptized precisely four weeks later. Her parents were indeed Chloe's great-grandparents. Chloe was ecstatic. She had made note of the year in which Emma's last picture has been taken. She would have been seventeen at the time. On a hunch, she decided to go through the marriage records of that year and the following year. She let out a small shriek of excitement. She discovered that Emma had married just one month shy of her eighteenth birthday to a young man by the name of Joaquim Jose Pereira. She decided to pursue her hunch further and check the baptism register for the following year and the year thereafter. She scoured the baptism register for two years as planned and upon finding nothing, went through records for three more years. The trail had gone cold.

As Emma paused to dwell on what she had successfully uncovered, she looked at her watch and realized that several hours had passed her by. She could not trespass on the good graces of Padvigar or the office assistant anymore. Chloe helped the young assistant put the heavy ledgers back in place and left after thanking her profusely.

When Chloe got back home, it was far past lunch time and she was famished. Thoughtful Angela had left her a portion of rice, prawn curry, mackerel recheado and tendli bhaji cooked to perfection in sweet, grated coconut. Chloe gladly wolfed it all down with her bare hands. Her fat-free, carb-free diet had been shelved into hibernation for the time being.

With a full belly and a contented mind, Chloe was able to take a much-deserved afternoon siesta. She had rarely had the luxury for the past few years. It served her well. When she awoke; she was hit by another brain wave. 'Chloe' the glamorous model had a massive following on social media. That very evening, she posted beautiful pictures that she had taken of her ancestral home thanks to her keen artistic eye. She added the picture of a seventeen-year-old Emma, with a tastefully crafted story. In the end, she asked anyone who knew about Emma's story or her whereabouts, to contact her.

Less than a week later, Chloe was ecstatic to find the reply that she had been looking for. A young teenager by the name of Felicity had written back, she had attached a wedding picture of her great-grandparents. It was indeed a picture of young Emma and a handsome young man. In all of the wedding pictures of the era that Chloe had encountered, the couple stood together in their finery, unsmiling. However, in this unique picture, the young couple was smiling happily as they gazed at each other.

Emma wore a simple white dress and carried a small bouquet of flowers. Chloe was struck with a feeling of déjà vu. The picture felt like that of her parents on their wedding day. Could that have been the reason why Emma was estranged from her family? Had she married against their wishes?

Felicity had provided a few details in her email like the fact that the family was now based in Toronto and that Emma was still alive and well. Felicity was an aspiring model who dreamt of making it big like Chloe. Most importantly, she could not wait to discover the nature of the connection between the photograph that Chloe had posted and her family.

A few months later…

Chloe fidgeted nervously with the strap of her handbag as she stepped into the foyer of the expensive restaurant in Toronto. Several men in smart suites turned to give her long, lingering looks. But she barely noticed. She had far more important things on her mind and butterflies in her stomach. She was here to reclaim a severed arm of her family.

In the months that followed their initial correspondence, Felicity had been instrumental in connecting Chloe with the rest of the family. Chloe learnt that Emma had indeed been cut off from her family for marrying against their wishes. She had led an adventurous life that led her first to Africa and then to Canada some decades later. She had borne one child, Elizabeth, who had in turn borne one child, Azalea, who had in turn borne Felicity, again an only child. Chloe had laughed at the strange coincidence. Emma had the opportunity to speak to all four generations of women in the months that had passed. They were thrilled to have found her and were eager to meet her in person.

As Chloe stood there and scanned the restaurant, she experienced emotions ranging from trepidation to excitement. A tall gangly young girl came towards her with outstretched arms and a wide smile. Chloe smiled back into the vivid eyes that greeted her – the eyes of Voiz Francisco Tomas Sousa.

2

A Groom for Alba

Alba was woken up from a deep sleep by her mother, Bella, vigorously shaking her shoulder.

'Utt gho!' she barked. (*Wake up!*)

Bella never spoke in a gentle tone anymore. Perhaps she had, when all her children were small. Alba could not recall. There were four of them children – Maria, Anthon, Jessy and Alba in that order. Alba opened her eyes and it was still dark all around. She knew that the time would be somewhere around 4 AM for this was the time when the household rose, or at least the women did. Her mother would let her lump of a brother sleep till 7 AM. But she would never have been spared the early hour especially since she was now the only remaining daughter in the house. Maria had been married off a couple of years earlier and Jessy was now working as a nanny for a family in Bombay. Bella did the cooking but left most of the other household chores to Alba. The men were not to be bothered of course. That was the way it was.

The fact was that Alba and her family was poor. At the time, they lived in a tiny rented house that boasted an even tinier verandah. Alba loved that house. She thought it made them all seem respectable, for the family had been living a nomadic life for years – moving from one small rented room to another. Alba's father did odd jobs for people such as replacing roof tiles and felling trees, as and when he could find the work. Unfortunately, he drank away all of his earnings. Her brother Anthon had two lazy eyes and had taken to the bottle like his father as soon as he reached adulthood. He worked for the local butcher, catching pigs for slaughter. Bella was therefore in the true sense of the word, the breadwinner of the family. She worked for the bhatkar as a domestic maid and also in their fields. She was tough as nails and was the only reason why a household burdened with alcoholism had not also succumbed to domestic violence. Her husband knew not to mess with his wife or expect a rupee of her wages, which went entirely into the running of her household. He had, one day, come home drunk and had been goaded by his drinking pals to use violence if necessary to extract money from his wife. He had raised his hand on Bella once. Before he knew it, she had hit him on the head with the blunt end of a khoitho and had promised him that she was not afraid to use the sharp end, if he did not behave. He had believed her. She had told him that he was lucky that she fed him and put a roof over his head and if that was not enough for him, he could leave and no one would miss him. He believed her again for it was the truth. Bella was never one to bluff.

Alba lit up the kerosene lamp fashioned out of an old glass bottle and rags. She needed to complete all of her chores before she left for her first day of work. The family had no electricity. They would therefore set and rise with the sun. Alba's parents were asleep by 8 PM and would rise just as early. Alba and Anthon would try to stay up a little longer than their parents and would be chastised by their mother for wasting kerosene.

Alba's first chore was fetching and filling water from the nearby well. She needed to ensure that the family had enough water to last them the entire day. She would carry two pots at a time to ensure that she completed the task in at least four to five trips. Next, she lit up a fire under a large pot in the backyard to heat water for their baths. She washed soiled clothes on the flat rock outside and spread them on ropes that were hung between coconut trees. She swept and mopped the house before she went to get ready herself. Her mother would have simultaneously cooked rice and 'saurakh' curry for the afternoon, along with a breakfast of chapatis. She would generally come back home to finish cooking and have lunch herself around noon. Anthon usually would be awake just in time to enjoy a hot breakfast and Alba would join him. But this day, Alba was nervous about her new job and could only eat a few bites.

When Alba turned seventeen, Bella decided that it was time for her to start working and supporting the family. Alba had dropped out of school a couple of years earlier after having flunked the ninth standard. Her older sister, Jessy had gone about things in pretty much the same way. She had been a little more fortunate to gain employment as a nanny for a family in Bombay. As for Alba, Bella had found out that the bhatkar's eldest son and his wife needed someone to look after their three-year-old daughter. She jumped at the opportunity and immediately offered up Alba's services. Alba would need to work between 8 AM and 6 PM and look after the child at the bhatkar's house while both her parents were away at work. The pay was not much but Bella was happy to have a daughter of hers work for the bhatkar.

Alba was jittery as her mother led her to the bhatkar's house.

"Baegin chol gho!" her mother demanded, "Bhatkanni ravlea." *(Hurry up! Bhatkanni is waiting.)*

Alba had only accompanied her mother there to help on odd jobs a few times before. She had worn one of her better dresses today, had used talcum powder and had washed her dusty slippers the night before. The bhatkar's house was palatial compared to their small home. Alba remembered thinking that the house her family lived in could fit into the kitchen alone. Bhatkar's house had electrical lights in all its rooms and they even had a couple of pedestal fans. Her mother had told her that bhatkanni had a cooking range that used gas and it came with an attached oven to bake cakes! Alba had been deeply impressed.

As they entered the house through the back door or dharvantto, Alba was in awe again even though this was hardly her first visit. Bhatkar was old but slender and tall with a head full of silver hair. He always wore knee-length cotton trousers and a cotton shirt along with flat, soft leather shoes in the house. Bhatkanni was a short, round woman who was clearly in command of the household and all those who worked for it. The old timers still referred to her as 'vhokol bai' – a title that had been bestowed upon her some thirty years before, when she had entered the house as a young bride. She now wore a simple cotton dress with her hair oiled, neatly parted and tied in a bun. She had a long golden chain around her neck, large gold earrings, and wore four gold bangles on her left hand. She was a mother of eight children, most of them now adults with only the youngest three still in college. The oldest son of the house was the only one of the children who was married and it was his daughter who would be Alba's young charge under bhatkanni's supervision.

'Bhatkanni, hem polem, Alba ailem', Bella said as soon as bhatkanni was in view. *(Bhatkanni, look, Alba's here.)*

Bhatkanni carefully regarded Alba before leading her to her daughter-in-law. Her name was Anita and all the servants in the house referred to her as 'Anita bai'. Anita bai's husband was 'Mario babu' and the little girl was Brinella, lovingly called 'Kuku' by everyone in the house. Kuku was an adorable child with wide eyes and straight shoulder-length hair in pigtails. Being the first grandchild, the little girl was pampered and she loved being the center of attraction.

After Anita bai and Mario babu left for work, Alba spent her first day with Kuku under the watchful eye of bhatkanni. At lunch, Kuku would be fed only by her grandmother so Alba took a quick trip home for lunch. A few days later, bhatkanni instructed Alba to stay and have lunch at the house, along with the other servants. Alba did not mind at all for the food was much better at bhatkar's house and she was always assured of a decent piece of fish or meat to go along with her rice and fish curry. In the evenings, she was always offered a loaf of bread and a cup of hot tea to dip it in. She would leave by 6 O'clock, which was the time by which Anita bai came home from work.

At three years of age, Kuku was quite a handful and had something of a temper. She would sometimes pull a fistful of Alba's hair in a rage. Alba was always careful about how she corrected Kuku. Anita bai had quite a temper herself and was very mindful of any complaints that Kuku might have about Alba. She would not hesitate in giving Alba an earful. As Kuku grew older, she was no longer in need of constant supervision and as a result, Alba was given other tasks such as washing and drying clothes. When Kuku started school, her parents would drop her off at school and Alba would collect her and bring her home by public bus.

Alba also began helping Bella with her chores at bhatkar's house. They would spread paddy on bamboo mats to dry and furrow the paddy bed with their feet. At the end of the day, the paddy had to be collected and stored again. Kuku would watch intently as Bella would hold a trough woven out of bamboo, full of paddy, over her head and let it fall in a carefully controlled shower, while Alba fanned wildly. She watched the useless empty husks being fanned away while the heavy good grain gathered in a conical pile at Bella's feet. Then, there were chilies or pieces of coconut kernel to dry, the latter would be crushed for oil.

In the summer, during the mango season, Alba and Bella would cover one of the storeroom floors with a bed of hay and lay rows and rows of mangoes upon it. These would be covered with another fine blanket of hay and left to ripen. Bhatkanni would generally instruct Bella and Alba on what needed to be done. She was kind to Alba and taught her how to embroider. But they would both make sure that Kuku was never too far out of sight. Anita bai did not appreciate Alba straying away from her child and would often obtain reports from Kuku.

Alba would religiously hand over half of her wages to Bella. She diligently saved whatever she could of the other half and was careful to hide the money well away from her father and brother. Alba had a dream. She wanted, above all, to marry. She was a very plain girl, but what she lacked in attractiveness she more than made up for in sheer grit and determination. She wanted to make a few gold ornaments for herself. Her mother had given the only gold she possessed, which was two gold bangles, to her eldest sister Maria. Alba also knew that she would need to pay for her own wedding. She would work and save as much as she could to realize her dream.

It took Alba, seven years to save enough, to make a gold chain for herself and an oval-shaped pendant with the letter 'A' engraved on it. That same year, Alba's family was evicted from their rental accommodation by the owners who decided to return to the house from abroad. Bella went to bhatkanni and pleaded with her for a piece of land on which the family could build a small house of their own. Bhatkanni had grown fond of Alba and knew that she was needed to take care of Kuku. The family was therefore permitted to use a small plot of land to build their own home.

A sturdy hut was all the family could afford. Bella's husband and son put in the manual labour, whereas Bella and Alba shelled out the cash for the building materials. The floor of the hut was plastered with cow dung by Bella who was elated that her family finally had a place of their own. She was overcome with gratitude to bhatkanni. Even Alba felt the force of this obligation – she would have to work for the bhatkar's family and take care of Kuku until Kuku was old enough to not need her anymore.

But Alba had wanted more of life. She wanted a husband and kids of her own and with the way things were, she worried that time was simply passing her by. Bella seemed to be uninterested in making her a match and there were no other elders or relatives in the family who could arrange a match. Alba had been bold enough to voice her concern to Bella on a few occasions, but Bella had not acknowledged her. Frustrated by her mother's indifference, Alba had requested her married sister Maria and Jessy in Bombay to help. She offered candles and prayers in church and prayed fervently for love.

Years passed. Alba had been working for the bhatkar family for a little more than a decade. Kuku was now a teenager and was quite responsible and independent. During this period, Alba's older sister Jessy had left her nanny job and managed to go to Dubai. There she'd met a man and married him and seemed to be very happy. This felt like a wake-up call to Alba. She decided to quit. This job had offered her security but it had enveloped her into a sheltered existence. She needed to get out. Bella was furious. But was also her mother and could not dissuade Alba from her plan, since she knew that she was of no help to her daughter in the matter of marriage. Anita bai was livid.

'Tumkam kitlem kelam ami!' she fumed. *(We have done so much for you!)*

But Alba was firm. Bhatkanni was far more sympathetic once she knew why Alba had decided to leave. Kuku was still at school when all this transpired. Alba decided it was better not to stay around for goodbyes. 'Kuku'k sang, bhatkanni', she said and left their house through the dharvantto.

Although Alba had not completed her schooling, she had a good grasp of the English language. She began checking the papers for vacancies and soon landed a job as a sales assistant in a wine shop in Mapusa. This meant a thirty-minute bus commute each way. She felt that her worldview was already widening. Her working hours were 9 AM to 6 PM and she was given limited time for bathroom breaks and lunch. But the pay was better. She even opened her first bank account at the ripe old age of twenty-eight. She was relieved that she would no longer have to hide cash at home.

Alba was barely into a year of her new job when her father passed away. Bella was shaken, even though she tried to put on a brave front. She relied entirely on Alba for funeral arrangements but was pleasantly surprised when her son Anthon volunteered to pitch in. Bella had continued to work at the bhatkars even though old age was catching up and she was not able to perform the more rigorous manual labour that she previously could. Alba was touched to see bhatkar and bhatkanni at the funeral. Anita bai, Mario babu and Kuku weren't in attendance and Alba hadn't expected them to be.

Seeing bhatkar and his wife at the funeral, made Alba think about the family with whom she had spent so many of the young years of her life. She wondered if Kuku, now almost a young adult, would even remember Alba when she was all grown up. Had all her years of service even made a little dent on Kuku's memory? She wondered about it at times for she was indeed quite fond of the little girl. Whenever Bella brought news about Kuku, Alba was always happy to listen.

The role of primary breadwinner had somewhat shifted to Alba. She knew that she had to be strong, especially for her mother. She still hoped to meet a good man, get married and start a family. Then the hand of fate made its move, one afternoon while Alba was at work. A young stranger stopped by the shop for some beer and then lingered on to speak to her. His name was Samuel and he was not originally from Goa. Over the next few weeks, he made several stops at the shop to speak to Alba, always in the afternoons when the shop's owner was away at lunch. He seemed genuinely interested in getting to know Alba and she began looking forward to seeing him. A relationship was blossoming and Alba felt elated at the prospect. She did not however speak about it to Bella or any of her siblings. She wanted to be sure of things before she did.

Samuel finally did ask Alba out. They went to inconspicuous little places for tea and never stayed out too late because Alba did not want her mother to get suspicious or interfere. It wasn't very long before Samuel declared his love for Alba and expressed his desire to marry her. He had a steady job but always wanted to work in the Gulf, earn a lot of money and then return to Goa in a few years, with a sizeable nest egg. With it, he would buy land and build a house and raise a family. He told Alba that he would have liked to take her along with him. She had told him that she had been a nanny and he had promised her that she would easily find such work in the Gulf that paid handsomely. He was just trying to save enough money to pay for his passage and now, for hers, as well. Alba immediately offered her savings, but he declined.

"I want to take care of you Alba," he said, "I will find a way for us."

A few days later, Samuel surprised Alba with a gold engagement ring, the best that he could afford at the time. Alba was ecstatic. Her dreams were finally within reach, all thanks to him. Alba responded with a grand gesture of her own. She withdrew all of her savings, all of the thirty thousand rupees she had spent years accumulating and presented it to Samuel. It was a start to help them both get on their way together. It was decided that Samuel would first go alone and send for her once he had settled himself. The two shared a tearful goodbye and Alba for once stayed out late with him.

Alba never heard from Samuel again. It took her several months to acknowledge that she had been duped. She was crushed and her faith was shattered. At thirty-six years of age, she feared that she might never recover from Samuel's betrayal. She quit her job at the wine shop as she could no longer stand the place. She found another job that was similar in nature and wages, at a nearby bakery. She shuddered at the thought of her mother or siblings finding out about what had happened.

Unfortunately, Alba's peace of mind was about to deteriorate further. In a surprising move, Anthon married and brought home a wife. Alba's home life became a misery. The hut was small and space was an issue. Resentment brewed and bubbled between Alba and her new sister-in-law. Bella chose not to interfere. Alba yearned for a home of her own. She finally fled to her sister Maria and begged her to accommodate her in exchange for a small rent and help around the house. Maria who was now widowed and living with her teenage son reluctantly agreed. Alba lived with them for a few months, but some misunderstandings cropped up and Alba was asked to leave. This time, she found a small room on rent that fit into her small budget.

Alba was alone and lonely. She felt that her life was a dull routine of work during the day and dreary nights in her small room. The only time she went out, was to church. Unfortunately, this too served as a pointed reminder about the family she had always wanted but did not have. Jessy was Alba's last remaining ally. Alba wrote to her and told her about everything, even about Samuel. Jessie, who was doing quite well for herself, was immediately sympathetic to Alba's plight. She knew well that she had been far more fortunate as compared to her siblings, especially her sisters. She and her husband had just recently bought a small plot of land for themselves back in Goa. They were already building a house. She wanted to help her little sister and offered her whatever little comfort she could, being so far away. She urged Alba to break her routine and go out. She even sent some money.

Alba was grateful to her sister for making her realise that now that she was on her own, she actually had the freedom to live her life. She no longer had to answer to her mother or account for every paise spent. She began making small attempts to lift her spirits. With the help of the money from Jessy, she treated herself to a few movies and new clothes. Although she succeeded, these experiences made her miss her mother and she decided to mend fences.

Alba visited her mother's place and took along some groceries and small gifts for her mother and sister-in-law. Her mother was overjoyed to see her and her sister-in-law was cordial as well. She was happy that she had visited because the visit had made her realise that moving out had been the right thing to do. As for her mother, she seemed to be alright too. As she prepared to leave, her mother said, "Rav bai. Kuku ielelem. Hem tuka soddun ghelam". (*Wait dear. Kuku had visited. She left this for you*).

Bella handed over Alba a wedding invitation. Alba was delighted. She clutched the envelope like a little treasure and hurried back to her room. She gently fingered the textured paper of the invitation and the gilded letters on them. Little Kuku was now all grown up and had invited her to her wedding. She had remembered. Alba had made a dent after all!

Alba attended only the nuptials. She knew she would feel out of place at the reception. She admired the way the church had been decorated with beautiful fresh white flowers on the altar and along the pews. She stared at Kuku, in her beautiful white dress in an attempt to absorb every plush detail. She looked around and spotted the bride's parents. Bhatkar had passed some years ago, but bhatkanni looked regal in a deep grey satiny dress with her white hair tied up in a bun as it always had been.

When the couple emerged from the church, she joined the line of guests waiting to wish them. She only had a small gift, a rosary, for Kuku. She held her breath when she faced the couple. Recognition immediately dawned on Kuku's face and she beamed. "Alba!" she cried, "I am so happy that you came!" She introduced Alba to her husband as the lady who had taken care of her during her childhood. Alba could not ask for more. She felt valued, as though she had made a significant difference in the world.

More good things followed. The tide had finally turned. Jessy found a match for Alba. The man, who was nearly fifty, was a widower. He was known to Jessy and her husband. He worked in Dubai and was a work colleague. She introduced him to Alba who was indeed careful to assess this time around.

The marriage was arranged. The groom-to-be would come down to Goa for the wedding, along with Jessy and her husband. Alba would set out for her wedding from Jessy's new house. After the wedding, she would travel to the gulf with her new husband and they would work together towards building a house and making a home of their own.

A little while later, Alba found herself knocking on Kuku's door. She had come to invite Kuku to her wedding. Kuku received her warmly. They sat and talked for quite a while. Kuku was thrilled that Alba was finally getting married. She had known that it was the reason why Alba had left all those years ago. She said that she would be very happy to attend Alba's wedding.

Alba's dream had finally come true. Better late than never.

3

Pao Ani Pizza

Philsu sat by the ancient bread-laden table and cracked her knuckles. It was a nasty old habit that took over during times of anxiety. How Anthony had hated it, whenever she repeated the habit. But no matter how many times he scolded her, Philsu could not seem to get over it. The unexpected memory of her son stilled Philsu instantly. She continued to gaze out of the wide-open front door and began praying silently in an attempt to soothe her soul.

It was late evening, and heaps of unsold pao lay neatly stacked on her table. Dozens of poies and khatre pao, now cool to the touch stared up at the tiled roof. Philsu was beset with worry and remorse. Earlier in the day, she had lost her last delivery boy. The old bicycle was leant against the side of the entrance wall, its tarp-bound basket gaping and empty.

'What a pitiful sight!' thought Philsu to herself. She felt like she had committed the most unforgivable act of treachery that day. For the first time in more than seventy years, bread had not been delivered to the homes of the bakery's customers that evening. Manu, her last delivery boy had left in a huff earlier in the day on the pretext that she made him work far too much whilst paying him far too little. She had known for some time that his brother had put up a shack and had invited Manu to join him in the business. He had just been bidding his time and looking for an excuse to quit. She shuddered at the thought of all her angry long-time customers who had been left with no bread for dinner. She felt that she had failed them. She felt extremely guilty.

Philsu was very familiar with guilt. It had been her only and constant companion for years. It still visited her regularly at the slightest provocation. It was with her today to stir up a hornet's nest of painful memories. She had always blamed herself for Anthony's death. Anthony, the older of her two sons, was the apple of her eye. What a beautiful child he had been! He had been lanky and fair, with brownish hair and large soulful eyes. One look and he could melt her heart. It was no wonder that she had spoilt him and fulfilled every whim – a motorcycle on his eighteenth birthday, branded clothing and a generous amount of pocket money. A widow for many years, she had been busy managing the bakery and raising two boys all on her own. How could she not have noticed when Anthony took to drugs? How could she have been so careless as to not warn him about drugs in the first place? How could she not have been suspicious of the company that he had begun to keep? These questions and so many more like them would plague her for the rest of her life.

Anthony had died of a suspected overdose. Philsu had been dumbfounded when it happened. In an attempt to compensate for her perceived failure with Anthony, she had gone overboard with Andrew. Andrew, her younger son was almost a decade younger than his elder brother. Her determination to save Andrew from a similar fate as his brother had made her paranoid and overbearing. It was no wonder that he had migrated to the UK as soon as he came of age. She'd felt that it had all been to escape her. Andrew's departure had added another rotten layer of grief and guilt to her already miserable existence. She felt that she had badly failed at being a mother. Now the only thing that she clung to, the only thing keeping her afloat, was the bakery that she had inherited from her late father.

Things had begun to go badly at the bakery as well. The cost of commodities had been increasing steadily but raising the price of bread was a very sensitive issue. The bakery just about broke even. She could not afford to pay her workers what they were being offered in other lines of work, such as in hotels, restaurants and the like. She had only three workmen now who were either nearing or past the standard retirement age. She needed someone younger to make the deliveries of bread twice a day.

Her bakery used a traditional wood-fired oven and obtaining firewood had become a major hassle. It was bad enough that she had to abandon the use of toddy in her bread in favour of ready-made yeast. Gone were the days when toddy had been readily available.

Her woes just seemed to be piling higher and higher. She sometimes wondered whether the bakery was still worth the effort and the agony. There was no one she could leave it to, no one she could pass the mantle to. She would have to either sell it or lease it out someday when she was too old and fragile to keep things going. Why not just do it now and live in some comfort? Was it her late father's legacy that she was trying to protect or perhaps she was not done punishing herself for having failed her children?

The evening had turned to night and the air was cool. A chilly November breeze blew into the doorway and Philsu shivered slightly. A few patrons had been in and out to buy her bread. She silently heard their grievances about the bread not being delivered to their homes and sincerely apologized for the inconvenience. Would they have understood her situation, if she had tried to explain it to them? Tomorrow, she would make Alfie deliver the bread on his scooter. The cost of fuel would only add to her money troubles, but what other choice did she have? Alfie was well over fifty, but he was the only other worker who knew all the routes and the houses where the bread needed to be delivered. She simply could not risk alienating her customers by letting them down again. She was deep in thought, mulling over the issue when she heard a gentle knock on the door frame. She looked up and found an elderly unkempt Caucasian man standing at her doorstep. He had long dark hair that was streaked with grey and tied into a messy ponytail. His greying beard was badly in need of a good trim.

"Scusi Madam," he said politely "How much for the bread?" He was staring at the bread in fascination. Then, he cautiously picked up one specimen each of the poie, khatro pao, kakonn, undo and four loaves of pao. He handed all of them to Philsu who wrapped them up in newspaper and handed over the parcel back to him. She was tempted to quote an exaggerated price to this foreigner but refrained from doing so. He paid her and said, "Grazie madam", before heading off. She was surprised to see that he had a bicycle with him. He placed the parcel of bread in a basket that was attached to the front of the bike and rode away with ease, even though he appeared to be well into his fifties. Philsu had never seen him before. He must be a tourist, she thought to herself and wondered how he had found his way to her bakery. She wondered if he had perhaps come to live somewhere nearby for the long term. She knew that many foreigners like him had taken up places on rent and stayed for months at a time.

He was back again the next day and this time he only picked up a few unde and poie. It seemed that he had decided on which were his favourites after having sampled all of the types of bread the previous evening. He was still as polite and courteous as he had been the previous evening.

Philsu had developed an aversion to foreigners after Anthony's death. During the police investigation, it had been revealed that his drug dealer had been a foreigner. The hippie-like appearance of this man did not help his case. Philsu viewed him with disdain and treated him with a distant and forced courtesy because he was a paying customer. He had continued to visit the bakery every evening at around the same time. Philsu began to expect his visits. More than a week later, he introduced himself to her as Alonzo. Philsu merely smiled and nodded but offered no information about herself in return. From her neighbours, she learnt that Alonzo had bought an old house in the vicinity. It had been abandoned by its previous owners a long time ago. He was an Italian, had no family to speak of and occupied his days painstakingly restoring the old house all by himself.

The ruined little house was transformed within a few weeks. He had even landscaped the neglected garden and the whole place looked spectacular. He even named it. The words 'Il Santuario' were carved on a rustic piece of wood that was nailed to the front gate post. Philsu thought that the little house looked better than it had even when it was occupied by the previous owners, some twenty years before. It was perhaps the degree of love and care with which Alonzo has restored the old house or perhaps his courteous manner that thawed Philsu's heart. She began exchanging pleasantries with him on his daily visits, in English that was as broken as his.

After several weeks, Alonzo requested Philsu to allow him a tour of the inner sanctum of the bakery. She agreed easily even though the request caught her by surprise. The old house was just a series of four rooms linked by a common passage. Every inch of the floor seemed to be covered in a fine layer of white flour especially as they moved towards the back of the house.

The last room of the house housed the wood-fired oven and was therefore the largest. The large oven with the earthen finish was dome-shaped with a rectangular opening above which hung a dim light bulb. The dough would be slid in and out using a wooden paddle with a long handle. The workbench that was used to shape the dough stood against the wall on the other side of the room. Flat metal trays, that were used to shape eight loaves of bread in two neat rows, were stacked in a corner of the worktable. Adjacent to it, lay a large wooden trough in which the dough was first kneaded before being transferred to the workbench. An ancient-looking back door led into a small backyard, where chopped firewood was arranged into orderly stacks. A door by the side of the oven led to a small kitchen and the washrooms. Sacks of wheat flour were housed in the pen-ultimate room, while the first two rooms that were closest to the front of the house served as living quarters. The second room was for the workers and the first room was for Philsu. A long floral-print curtain divided Philsu's room into two sections. The section that contained the front door had a table for bread to be displayed, while Philsu's private quarters were on the other side of the curtain.

Alonzo nodded wordlessly to Philsu as she took him around the house. The three workmen who remained with her were surprised to have a visitor. But he dissipated their discomfort by enthusiastically nodding and smiling at them while clasping their hands in firm handshakes. At the end of the tour, Alonzo declared in a loud voice that he loved the bakery.

"I want to make pizza in this oven for all of you!" he boomed. "I bring all the ingredients; you just help me with the dough and the oven."

Philsu gave her workers a panicked look. "Kitem korunk sodta, tho?" *(What does he want to do?)*

Alfie ventured a response. "Pizza", he said.

"Ah, ah!" the three workmen said and nodded in unison. "Yes, yes!" Alfie enthusiastically offered. Alonzo clapped his hands in delight. He bade them farewell and headed to the front door, Philsu in tow. She remained silent and was still very surprised at what had just transpired. She was still quite uncertain of his offer but did not have the heart to retract Alfie's invitation. Alonzo left and she hurried back to the oven room to scold Alfie for his thoughtlessness.

Several hours later, that same night, there was a commotion at the bakery. Alfie suffered from a massive stroke that left him lifeless and drooling on the kitchen floor. Philsu and her two other workmen immediately called an ambulance and rushed him to the hospital. Philsu insisted on accompanying him. He had been a loyal employee for almost two decades and she felt that she needed to be by his side. Alfie had no immediate family, just a few distant relatives, who Philsu barely knew.

At the hospital, it was revealed that Alfie had suffered from a hemorrhagic stroke that had paralyzed his right side. He had been placed in the ICU for the night and Philsu sunk into gloom. She wondered whether he would fully recover and gain movement on his right side. "Only time will tell", the doctor had told her. Philsu knew that she would need to raise the money to pay the hospital bill. She decided not to think about the hospital bill until morning, nor about the fate of the bakery nor about what would become of all of them. Maybe it was time to stop fighting the tide and just go with the flow like everyone else. So many traditional bakeries had simply wound up their operations and leased out the premises to people from neighbouring states. It was the easy way out. Perhaps Alfie's stroke would become the straw that broke the proverbial camel's back. Philsu closed her eyes and leaned against the cool wall until her tumultuous thoughts were overcome by sheer exhaustion and she drifted into a semi-conscious dream-like state of sleep.

The empty corridors of the hospital came back to life early the next morning. Philsu was awakened by the sound of strangers milling about the hospital. A newborn baby wailed somewhere in the distance. It made her feel ancient. The cry was a poignant reminder of a stage of life that she had left far behind her. She'd decided to get up and go find the doctor to get an update on Alfie's condition when she noticed a shaggy long-haired figure walk towards her with a familiar gait. She adjusted her spectacles and was pleasantly surprised to see Alonzo walking towards her. She wondered what he was doing at the hospital so early in the morning. He came up to her and said, "Madame, I find out about Alfie. I am so sorry. Please tell me, is there anything I do to help?" Philsu was overwhelmed with gratitude.

"Thank you", she said in a coarse voice, glad that she was no longer alone.

Alonzo accompanied her to the doctor. The situation was grim but Alfie could recover slowly provided he had a lot of help and physiotherapy. Alonzo insisted that Philsu go home, while he stayed at the hospital. He would stay there until evening when she would be back to relieve him. Philsu was so grateful to this stranger who had become her angel. In the days to come, Alonzo would go out of his way to help her with Alfie's recovery. They took turns staying at the hospital and Philsu roped in the other two workmen to help out as well.

Alonzo went from being a customer and an acquaintance to a good friend. She had not had one in a long time. They talked to each other often and swapped life stories. They both had more in common than they had imagined. Alonzo had at one point been a very successful architect back in Italy. He said that he'd had it all until he had lost it all in the blink of an eye. He too had lost his only son, a teenager, in a road accident. It had been the kind of devastation that in all his privileged life, he had never imagined existed. His marriage had unraveled, and he had ultimately given up everything, his career, his house, his car, to become a wanderer. He admitted that he had no idea whether his travels were an escape or a quest for a higher truth. He had travelled extensively in the orient and after a few years, he had landed in Goa. When he had first seen the old house that he had purchased, it had awakened a part of him that he had thought was lost forever. It had made him want to create again. He'd bought the house and property and had tied himself to this place for the foreseeable future or at least until the grief in him rested in stillness like a wounded beast.

Philsu had decided that Alfie would recuperate at the bakery since it was the only home he had known for years. She tried to make him as comfortable as possible, she had hired a part-time nurse and a physiotherapist visited regularly. The hospital bill and all related expenses were funded by the money she had gotten after selling two of her gold bangles. The bakery still functioned but she still had not managed to find a replacement for Alfie who would make house deliveries as well. Alonzo once again came to her rescue and offered to work part-time in the bakery. "Now that I have finished the house, I have nothing else to do all day! Please let me help you! You will be doing me a favour." he pleaded. When Philsu had expressed her reservations and more importantly her inability to pay him a commensurate wage, he dismissed her concerns by saying, "Oh! Please don't let the way I look fool you." Then he had whispered conspiratorially, "I am very rich!" Philsu believed him and accepted his offer of help gratefully. How could she turn away this angel who God had sent to her, in her hour of need?

It turned out that in his former life, Alonzo had loved to cook and bake. "Had I not become an architect, I would have become a chef!" he joked. He patiently learnt his chores and even offered to deliver the bread to people's homes on the old bicycle. "This is too much!" Philsu had expressed. She felt like she was taking advantage of his kindness, but he assured her that she was not. He assured her that in fact, she had given him a sense of renewed purpose. He wanted to be of help for as long as he could.

Alfie's condition was improving by the day, and this gave Philsu hope. And of course, Alonzo had taken over the delivery of bread and had managed to learn most of the routes. Things were getting back to normal. But she knew that in a month or so when they had all struggled with Alfie's ailment, she had lost several of her customers. She wondered how she could win them back.

One afternoon, she was mulling this over at her old spot on the bread table when she was summoned. "Bai gho!" one of her workmen called to her from the oven room. She hobbled to the back of the house to find Alonzo and the two workmen huddled together at the workbench, admiring a large steaming hot pizza that was fresh from the oven. It was lunchtime! They savoured the pizza. Alonzo had finally delivered on the promise he had made to them some weeks ago. He had made the tomato sauce from scratch, used special cheese, and added vegetables and olives. The hot pizza tasted like nothing that Philsu has tasted before. "I told you that I could have been a chef," Alonzo exclaimed between mouthfuls, delighted with the expressions on their faces. Philsu's eyes lit up with inspiration and that was how the widely acclaimed artisanal bakery 'Pao ani Pizza' was born.

4

Casa Rosa

Omi drooled at the sight before him. He adjusted his gold-rimmed sunglasses as he surveyed the neglected plot of land that stretched out before him. 'By God, it's perfect!' he thought to himself. Wild and overgrown, it was not much to look at, but hidden behind all the vegetation was a gold mine! It was rectangular and bound on two sides by the public road. The third edge abutted a hillock, and the fourth edge adjoined another plot of land which was inhabited for on it stood a small house with a 'Tulas' out front. The thick and overgrown vegetation was fenced in by high walls trimmed with intricate stone latticework which was crumbling in a few places. Omi could see the ruins of a house from where he stood. A long balcony wrapped itself around three sides and a long row of stairs flanked on either side by stone seats, led to the main door. A tall imposing wrought iron gate enclosed the compound wall and cast a vivid shadow on the roadside. A marble plaque on one of the formidable gate posts bore the name 'Casa Rosa'.

Omi decided to walk along the accessible boundaries of his newly discovered gold mine. He couldn't wait to report his finding to Sunny Bhai. It was just what Sunny was looking for, for his new luxury condominium project. The little village in which the plot was situated was the up-and-coming 'hot' place to have a home in Goa. The hamlet was ideally situated close to town and was already swarming with all these high-profile artsy types – musicians, artists, actors, poets, and authors. To live in this place meant sharing a haven with the 'in' crowd and builders like Sunny Bhai could barely keep up with the demand. That's where people like Omi came in – people who did not mind getting their hands dirty for a piece of a very lucrative pie.

Omi had known Sunny since childhood. Sunny had been like a big brother to him. Omi had worshipped the ground that Sunny walked on until he had left home to make his fortune. However, before leaving, Sunny had promised Omi that he would come back for him one day. For several years thereafter, Omi had faithfully waited. Omi had always been as resourceful as he had been ambitious. He established himself as a real estate broker and made a decent living out of it. He was blessed with a glib tongue and easily developed the ability to close deals. He married his childhood sweetheart Sumi against his parents' wishes. She belonged to a lower caste than him, but he had been determined to have her join his large joint family. Predictably, Sumi's in-laws treated her like a low life. She was miserable. Omi knew that the time had come for him to strike out on his own, but he had little idea of how to do so. Then like the proverbial knight in shining armour, Sunny reappeared in town. Only this time he was not the ordinary boy next door but a glamorous businessman who glided into town in a posh car. He had on his arm, a glamorous wife who went by the name of Lucky.

Sunny embraced Omi as his long-lost brother. He offered him an once-in-a-lifetime opportunity. "Come with me to paradise and help me in my real estate business," he said, "I guarantee that in a few years you will be a rich man!"

Omi thanked his Gods and his lucky stars. 'Paradise', he realized was Goa. He packed his bags and left his hometown along with Sunny, with Sumi firmly by his side.

Upon arriving in Goa, Sunny gave Omi and Sumi a fully furnished two-bedroom flat to live in. It was theirs to reside in for the duration of Omi's employment with Sunny's construction firm. Omi was also given a motorcycle and a monthly salary. His new job required him to draw upon his previous experience in real estate. His responsibilities included scouting for neglected land, investigating its ownership and history, and creating the necessary documentation so that it could be acquired by Sunny constructions. These responsibilities were his to fulfill by using any means necessary. It all amounted to theft. If the owners wizened up to what was happening to their land and tried to sue, the process was long drawn, and things were almost always resolved through a settlement which was a fraction of what Sunny would ultimately make. Omi received a handsome commission based on the market value of the land if he did his job right. He could rake in the dough. Sunny had indeed delivered on his promise. In Omi's eyes, there was no question of right and wrong, because he was simply an agent. The owners were entirely to blame for such criminal neglect of their property. If it was not Omi, it would have been someone else who took advantage of their apathy. Omi was not alone in these endeavours of course; Sunny had built himself quite a team which included Goan lawyers who were well acquainted with Portuguese era law and the right government officials who had access to land records that dated back to Portuguese colonial times. They were all in it together, all in for the money.

The status of Omi and Sumi as a couple in society had been elevated, all thanks to Omi's new line of work. After closing just a couple of deals, Omi had been promoted from being the owner of a two-bedroom flat to a three-bedroom flat, from a motorcycle to a fancy car. Omi lavished his wife with expensive gifts, weekend getaways, meals in expensive restaurants and the works. She soon became the envy of all her in-laws back home in their cramped family dwelling. She enjoyed the feeling. It was sweet revenge for all the hardship that they had put her through. Sunny often invited Omi and Sumi to lavish parties that he threw for clients, investors, government officials and the like.

During these gatherings, the wives would always retreat to their own space while the men talked shop. Sumi was in awe of Lucky. She felt awkward and a bit inferior to Sunny's glamorous wife. However, Lucky wasted no time in taking Sumi under her wing. She introduced the small-town girl to the world of beauty spas and salons, designer labels and gourmet food.

Pretty soon, Omi and Sumi became addicted to the good life. They could not imagine going back to their small-town, small-time roots.

As Omi walked along the edge of the road surveying the narrow side of the rectangular plot, he noticed the elderly man from the house next door staring at him. Once the man ascertained that he had Omi's attention, he boldly walked towards Omi and said Hello. Omi quickly sized up the older man – probably in his sixties, a local for sure. Not wanting to draw unwanted attention and painfully aware that he did not blend into the neighbourhood, Omi pretended to be a tourist.

"Oh, Hello uncle", he greeted the man warmly and then continued his greetings in Hindi. In the brief moment when they exchanged pleasantries, Omi introduced himself as 'Omi, a tourist', whereas the older man introduced himself as 'Govind'. Omi wasted no time in putting up his façade. He told Govind that he was very interested in Goa's unique old houses for their Indo-Portuguese architecture. He pointed to Casa Rosa even though it wasn't clearly visible due to all the wild vegetation and went on about it with the air of an expert. He finally concluded that it must have been a beautiful house in its heyday. Govind intently listened to Omi's soliloquy and finally nodded his head in agreement. "Ah yes," he admitted, "It was a very beautiful house, and the owner always maintained it well."

Omi pounced at the opening that Govind had provided, "So what happened, Uncle? Where are the owners?"

Govind contemplated a little before answering, "The owner is a good friend of mine. He is settled in Australia. His mother lived here till she died more than ten years ago. The house is named after her 'Casa Rosa'. She was an avid gardener, and her garden was always filled with the most beautiful roses." He explained wistfully.

"Oh, so sad, uncle", Omi went on, "Isn't her son coming back?"

"He keeps saying that he will eventually come back, but he hasn't so far. The poor old lady died waiting for him to come home." Govind smiled sadly.

"So, is he in touch with you these days, Uncle?" Omi feigned innocence.

"Yes, now and then," Govind replied.

An involuntary frown appeared on Omi's face. 'This might be a serious problem', he thought to himself. He decided to quickly change tact.

"What about you, Uncle? How is your family?" he inquired.

"Oh, it's just my wife and me in the house right now. Our sons both work in Mumbai." Govind replied.

"That's good, Uncle. Thank you for your time, Uncle. I'll get going now." Omi said with his hand folded into a Namaste.

As he walked away, Omi couldn't help but worry. The old man definitely presented a problem. Maybe they could pay him off. They needed to quickly take care of the paperwork and begin construction immediately. They would worry about settling if the need arose. Their team was well-equipped to handle such eventualities. Anyway, in his experience, owners who settled abroad lacked the resolve to put up much of a fight to protect their ancestral land and were more than happy to accept a quick and fat settlement. This place was too good to give up. He would talk to Sunny about it and leave it to his expertise in these matters.

Govind watched Omi as he ambled towards his car. He shook his head in disgust. He must have been the fifth person to inquire about Norbert's property. He was well aware of the type of nefarious land-grabbing activities that were going on around him. He had tried to reach Norbert several times to warn him but had failed. He would try again. He had known Norbert since childhood. Not only were they neighbours, but they had both been born barely a month apart. They had played together and attended the same school and college together after which life had taken them on separate paths.

Norbert followed in his father's footsteps and went on to become a sailor whereas Govind went on to take a government job like his father. Norbert had steadily risen in the ranks until he became a captain. His trips back home trickled into nothing when he decided to leave Goa for greener pastures leaving behind his mother, Rose. Aunty Rose, as Govind had always referred to her, held a special place in his heart. She had been tall, regal and elegant just like a queen, and just as warm-hearted. She had tutored Govind in English at no cost to his parents. He owed his fluency in the language to her efforts. In a way, he felt that he owed his success in his career to her. Consequently, he'd always looked out for Aunty Rose while Norbert was away. The lady had remained fiercely independent till her end, but she could always rely on Govind if something was ever amiss. She was accustomed to being on her own. She had lost her husband quite young and had doted on her only child, her son. When he had left her too, she did not falter and steadied the course that lay ahead.

Govind could barely recall Norbert's father, Uncle Robert. But he had a distinct impression that he had been a good-looking fellow. Robert and Rose had made a handsome couple and at a time when folks lived frugally, they lived well thanks to Robert's sailing career. Govind could remember being in awe of their immaculate home no matter how often he visited. He remembered the sparkling chandelier in their hall, the little porcelain figurines that Aunty Rose was always dusting and most of all he remembered the roses. Their home was always filled with vases of them. Aunty Rose was an avid gardener and grew several varieties of Roses, but always in hues of pink and red only. Govind remembered how his mother always had a rose in her hair thanks to that wonderful garden. Even after all the years that had passed, the smell of roses still evoked in him powerful memories of childhood which seemed to cut across time. He would look at the house and the sorry state that it was in now and shudder in sorrow and humility at what time and neglect could reduce beauty and pride to.

The land sharks were circling, and he hoped that Norbert would heed his call. Norbert had always spoken about growing old at his parent's house in his beloved Goa. But his apathy towards his mother had made Govind wary of his best friend's intentions. Perhaps he would be happy to sell it off at a good price. But an inane sense of loyalty towards Aunty Rose made Govind want to at least try and reach out to Norbert.

Just a couple of days from when he had first seen him, Govind found Omi lurking around the old house again. As soon as he spotted Govind, he audaciously made his way towards him carrying what appeared to be a large box of sweets.

"Arre Uncle, Namaste. How are you?" he panted as he reached Govind's doorstep and took a seat on the stone sopo without being invited to.

"A small gift for you," he said and offered Govind the box of sweets.

Govind politely declined. He explained that both his wife and he suffered from diabetes. Omi insisted once more, but Govind was firm. Not wanting to offend or alienate, Omi set the box aside.

"Uncle, I have a favour to ask," Omi said nervously, clearing his throat. "I have fallen in love with that plot of land next to your house. I want to build a house for myself there. Can you help me to acquire it? I will pay you a very good commission."

Govind's face was impassive for a second. Then he quickly shook his head.

"Na baba na," he said, "I don't want to get involved with the sale of that land and that house. Tem pensaolem ghor."

"What does that mean, uncle?" Omi inquired.

"It means that the house is cursed because its late owner was too attached to it. She will never let it go. You see she died waiting for her son to come back home. She will never let it go," Govind repeated the last statement to emphasize his point.

"Achha," Omi nodded. He had the answer he was looking for all along. Govind could not be bought. It was time for plan B.

"I will take your leave now, Uncle," he said with folded hands. Govind simply nodded and watched him leave. He wondered whether the threat of a curse was enough to keep the oily agent away and buy some time to locate Norbert. He hoped to God that it was indeed enough.

Omi walked away a little skeptical about Govind's claim. He believed in the spirit world but that was hardly reason enough to let a fortune slip through his fingers. The day was overcast. It was the first weekend of June, the onset of the monsoon. He had plans to go clubbing that night along with Sumi, Sunny, and Lucky. Sunny loved to drive his imported SUV in the rain under the cover of darkness. It would be the perfect night for the foursome to take a long drive and visit the site with no one around. He had scouted the place some more. The streetlights worked fine. He had also managed to pry open the heavy wrought-iron gate and find a narrow path that led to the front of the ruined old house. Yes indeed, he would show Sunny his new find tonight.

It was almost 2 AM and eerily quiet when the group drove up to the side of the plot. Sunny was in the driver's seat while Omi sat shotgun beside him. Their wives were busy chatting away in the back seat. Sunny shushed up both of them. It had begun to drizzle lightly. The moon hid behind the cloud cover, but the dim streetlights were all they needed. Sunny and Omi got out of the car and their wives followed. Sunny warned them both to remain silent. They obediently tailed their husbands as Omi took the lead and directed them all past the heavy gate and onto the narrow pathway.

"Wah!" Sunny exclaimed as he patted Omi's back in appreciation. Omi grinned from ear to ear, happy to have pleased his big brother and boss. The undergrowth was too wild and wouldn't permit any further exploration into the property. But Sunny reckoned that this one was a winner. They would visit again in daylight but only after having notified their lawyers to begin their investigation and proceedings. Satisfied that they had seen as much as they could that night Sunny led everybody out and into the car. Once the car started moving, Sunny and Omi began an animated discussion about various construction possibilities. Their wives for once were listening intently. At some point, Omi joked about the possibility of the property being cursed and laughed out loud. Sunny joined him. But their wives widened their eyes in concern.

"Be careful, Sunnyji! What if it is really true and brings bad luck to all of us?" the normally sedate Sumi spoke up. Lucky chimed in, in agreement.

"Ladies, relax, okay?" Sunny threw up his hands off the steering wheel, "Do you know just how much I would have lost by now if I believed in every ghost story?" he exclaimed. "All these old plots and houses have some story or the other attached to them. It all means nothing in the end. Have you suffered from any bad luck?" he chastised them both. They both sat silently contemplating, while Sunny changed the topic and began a fresh discussion with Omi.

Less than a week later Sumi and Lucky tested positive for dengue fever. While both their wives recovered from bouts of high fever and intense body aches, Omi and Sunny had lunch together in Sunny's office.

"I just don't understand how both of them came down with dengue at the same time! Are they sisters or what?" Omi wondered out loud.

"Maybe they both got bitten by the same mosquito!" Sunny joked.

"The last time they were both together was when we went clubbing that weekend, remember? And after that, we visited that new site…My God! Do you think…" Omi paused mid-sentence.

"You mean that supposed curse on that house? Come on! That's nonsense." Sunny vehemently refuted.

"Hmm..you are probably right. But it's still a hell of a coincidence." Omi countered.

"That's exactly what it is, my friend. Don't jinx things for us with such talk." Sunny warned.

Omi was quick to change the subject. He reminded Sunny that they needed to visit the site with their main investor. Sunny brightened up at the idea. They contemplated making it a day trip. But Omi was wary of Govind always turning up. He did not want some unwarranted remark spooking their investor who was known to be very superstitious. They agreed on another night trip and set a date a couple of days later.

On the day in question, Sunny and Omi picked up their VIP guest, Tiku, from the five-star hotel they had put him up in. Tiku moved around in the same circles as Sunny. In other words, he was as shady as they came. He had made his fortune money laundering but the real estate market in Goa was looking awfully plum to pass up on.

It had been a dry evening when the trio had started out. But the moment they reached their destination, thick monsoon clouds had descended upon the sky and had begun emitting brief flashes of white light. It was mild lightning without any thunder but the wind had started to gather momentum. They decided to keep the trip as brief as possible to avoid the worst of the thunderstorm. They ushered Tiku through the gate and into the narrow clearing in front of the house. He stood with his hands on his ample hips, chewing the last of his paan whilst gazing up at the house.

"So, what is the name of this place again?" He inquired.

Omi was quick to answer, eager to please. "Sir, Casa Rosa. It was named after its last owner who it seems had a beautiful rose garden."

Suddenly the night sky was engulfed in white light and thunder and Tiku straightened his back in fright. The lightning had illuminated a white figure inside the house that vanished as soon as the sky grew dark again. The wind grew strong, and the house began emitting ghostly howling noises.

"Baba re," Tiku muttered just as there was another flash of lightning that made the white figure appear once again inside the house. Sunny and Omi who had also witnessed the horror, stood rooted to the ground in shock and fear. Tiku began shaking with fear. This pulled Sunny and Omi out of their trance. They quickly grabbed Tiku by his arms and dragged him out of the compound and into their car.

Back at his hotel, Tiku calmed down only after being plied with copious amounts of hard liquor. He demanded to know whether the old house was haunted. Sunny put up a brave front. But Tiku could not be placated. He threw an angry fit that made Sunny and Omi grovel. Omi spilt the beans. Tiku was furious that he had been kept in the dark about the ominous history of the house. He had always steered clear of anything associated with dark energy. He was already seriously considering withdrawing his investment from the project. Sunny and Omi pleaded with Tiku to give them another chance. Sunny reminded him of the potential profit from a project on the site which was prime real estate. He assured Tiku that there was no curse, no restless spirit. It had just been the rough weather that night and the alcohol that they had consumed earlier in the evening, which must have played tricks on their minds. He suggested that they visit the site in broad daylight. He was absolutely certain that everything would be clear in the light of day. He spoke and spoke till he was blue in the face and till Tiku was too exhausted to refute his arguments. Tiku had finally relented, and Sunny wasted no time in making plans for a day trip with Tiku the very next morning.

It was mid-morning when Sunny and Omi treated Tiku to a hearty brunch. They tried to gauge his mood and it seemed that the negative energy from the night before had mostly dissipated. They set out for the site. The sky was grey with rain clouds. Omi had hoped that old man Govind wouldn't be about to notice their foray into the abandoned plot. But he had no such luck. As usual, Govind was securely perched on the sopo of his balcony intently reading the newspaper. The trio entered the gate as quietly as possible on Omi's advice. They were immediately struck by a strong floral fragrance. It was the heady perfume of roses. They stepped into the clearing in front of the house and saw that roses were blooming everywhere, small and large, in varying shades of pink and red. They were astonished. Even though they had visited at nighttime before, they were certain that the flowers had not been there, neither had their overpowering scent. Now they seemed almost eerie and their colours looked vividly bright against the grey sombre atmosphere.

Suddenly it began blowing strongly and the house began emitting howling noises again. Instinctively the three of them took a step back and landed in a tangle of rose bushes with sharp thorns. They lost their footing and fell deeper into the bramble. The more they tried to stand and untangle themselves, the more ensnared they became. It seemed as though the thorny bushes were holding them down. Sunny managed to tear himself away and stand up. He immediately pulled up Omi and together they heaved the bulky Tiku onto his feet. Their faces and arms were badly scratched and bleeding. As soon as he was on his feet again, Tiku turned and ran. The other two followed him in a hurry. They ran past Govind who stood rooted to his spot astonished at the sight and smell of roses. He watched the three men jump into their car and speed away. Govind did not know for how long he stood there in amazement. The fragrance of roses had brought on an avalanche of memories. He could picture the ruined house in its former glory with Aunty Rose in the garden, bent over a rose bush, pruning shears in hand. Slowly he turned around and walked home.

Govind slumped back on the cool stone seat of his balcony. He had known all about Omi's clandestine visits to the old house. He had eavesdropped on most of their conversations and had made up the story of the pensao. He had hung a white bedsheet inside the house in the hope that it would scare them off and buy him some more time to reach Norbert. He knew that the intricate stone lattice work near the roof produced howling noises when a strong wind passed through them. But he could not explain the sudden appearance of roses from rose bushes that he did not even know survived after years of neglect. He felt goose bumps creep along both his arms. His phone rang and he nearly jumped out of his seat.

"Hello," he muttered still dazed.

"Hello Govind!" a familiar voice replied, "It's me, Norbert."

"Norbert?" Govind stammered, "You better come home now. Aunty Rose is still waiting…"

5

Avarenta

Rhea sat down in a huff as her mother, Rachel, busied herself around Rhea's room. She watched helplessly as Rachel carefully slid down the medium-sized suitcase from its storage space, wiped it clean and heaved it with a thud onto Rhea's bed. "Please start packing, Rhea", Rachel sternly instructed her daughter. "Your flight leaves at 7 AM tomorrow, so you need to wake up at 5." Rhea glared at her mother whilst seething with anger. 'How can she do this to me?' she glowered. But after several rounds of screaming matches, over the past couple of days, she felt drained of all the fight in her. Now residual anger was all that she had left and she held on to it tightly. It had become her crutch. Rachel threw her daughter a final loaded look and left the room, closing the door behind her. Rhea let out a long, frustrated sigh. It was as though she had not taken a breath for all of the time that her mother had been in her room.

At seventeen, Rhea was very pretty, stylish and hugely popular not only among her friends' circle but also on social media where she could boast of a relatively large number of followers. At school, she only put in the bare minimum amount of effort that it took to just make the grade. She knew that she could do better if she just tried, but her heart simply wasn't in it. She spent every cent of her pocket money on clothes, shoes, accessories and makeup. Her favourite place to be was the neighbourhood mall and to her being popular was as important as being young.

Her parents had always been generous with money. But of late, it seemed that they had begun to tighten their purse strings. It had all started with their neighbour, aunty Becky and her big mouth. Rhea thought to herself angrily. Why in the world did that darned woman have to interfere in her life? She had only caught a small fragment of what must have been a very long conversation between aunty Becky and her mother. But it was enough to understand how that tiresome woman must have poisoned her mother's mind. "You spoil Rhea too much..she lacks focus and direction..how will she get a good job…she has expensive tastes…blah blah blah." She'd gone on and on. "Every woman needs to be independent, just take my case.." she'd said. 'Your case? My foot!' Rhea fumed. Not every woman would end up a bitter divorcee like aunty Becky. She probably deserved it, she thought angrily.

After that little chat, it seemed like Rachel had begun closely watching Rhea's expenses. And it was unfortunate that unaware of her mother's gaze on her, Rhea had 'borrowed' her father's credit card and splurged on a dress and the works for her college socials. Rachel had exploded! 'But mummy, it was the last year of junior college!' Rhea had tried to explain in vain but Rachel would have none of it. She had grounded Rhea and practically chained her to her study table until the end of her final exams. And now that exams were over she was hell-bent on banishing Rhea to some obscure village in Goa.

Rachel had decreed that Rhea would have to spend her summer vacation with her maternal grandmother. How would she ever get through it? The village as Rhea remembered, was beautiful but sleepy with nothing interesting to see or do. She took some solace in the fact that her friends had oohed and aahed about her vacation in Goa. She did not dare tell them that she would not be living in some gorgeous beach-side resort but in a two-hundred-year-old house in an interior village, where landlines still functioned as the predominant mode of communication. She would need to somehow make the place look really cool in the pictures she took for her social media account.

"Get going, Rhea!" Rachel barked after having poked her head into Rhea's room again. Rhea knew only too well that her mother was a formidable opponent. Upon hearing of her banishment to her grandmother's place, Rhea had pleaded and cried until she was blue in the face, but her mother had not budged. Even Rhea's indulgent father had not been able to get a word in. Rhea resigned herself to packing for the vacation that she had come to liken to a sentence. 'Nothing fancy,' she had decided, just the basic jeans and t-shirts. As an afterthought, she threw in a couple of plain dresses that she would wear for Sunday mass. She was told that the village padvigar did not approve of jeans, informal or revealing clothing being worn to church. 'How ridiculous!' Rhea thought, 'was that place still stuck in medieval times?' She was careful to pack her vanity kit which contained among other things no less than twenty-one shades of nail polish. She enjoyed grooming herself and she loved changing the shade on her nails several times a week. After she'd finished packing, she laid back on her bed, curled up alongside her suitcase and drifted off to sleep. She'd left all the lights on.

At 5 AM Rachel tugged at Rhea's blanket to wake her up. To Rhea, it seemed like she had barely slept at all. She was sullen all through the process of getting ready to leave. She deliberately didn't say a word to both her parents, even though her mother shot out instructions at her like a drill sergeant. When coaxed for a reply, Rhea merely grunted. She felt bad about her father though. She could see that he was truly sorry to see her go. He tried to make small talk all the way, as he drove her to the airport. When it was time to leave him at the airport, she finally put him out of his misery and properly said her goodbyes.

The flight was a short one, barely an hour. Rhea settled into her window seat. Dawn had broken and the sky was filled with the soft, warm light of a new day. She let her mind wander back in time. She rarely saw her maternal grandmother. 'Nana' as she was called by Rhea and her other cousins. Visits were an annual ritual, generally for a few days close to Christmas.

'Avarenta', Rachel had at times called her mother. It was Portuguese for miser. "Your nana does not like to spend money," she had told Rhea. Rachel narrated stories of her frugal childhood when she and her sisters were stitched only one new dress each, once a year. The dress had to see them through all of the special occasions throughout the year including weddings, various feasts, Christmas and Easter. Nana's younger sisters would also send them their hand-me-downs. Even Rachel who was the eldest could not escape wearing hand-me-downs.

There was one of Rachel's stories that particularly stood out in her memory. Nana had a younger sister who was settled in London. She would sent down little parcels of goodies for her siblings back in Goa, once or twice a year through acquaintances travelling down to Goa. The prized parcels would contain tinned ham, cheese and chocolates which would have to be carefully rationed. Nana would hide these little goodies like gold deep inside her massive wardrobe which she always kept locked. On one occasion, nana received two parcels from her sister. One was for her younger brother John and the other was for her. The visitor had been in too much of a hurry to visit Uncle John personally and requested nana to deliver it on his behalf. It seems that Uncle John was terribly disappointed with his parcel upon receiving it and wrote all about it to his little sister in London. He claimed that she had sent him an expired tin of cheese. The sister was very upset and confused about the whole situation and rather hurt by the accusation. It was only then that nana had come clean and revealed that she had switched the tin of cheese with one from her precious hoard. The incident had become one of Rachel's favourite jokes with her siblings, about their mother.

Rhea smiled at the memory. She remembered how her mother often reminded her of how fortunate she was not to have a tight-fisted mother like her nana. But now it seemed, that mama too had become as tightfisted as nana, at least when it came to Rhea. Rhea tsked aloud and shook her head at the thought. Her allowance had been drastically reduced to a fraction of its former glory. Her parent's credit cards were now completely off-limits.

The amount she had been given to last her through this so-called vacation had been laughable, but she had been in no position to do so and had meekly accepted it without any strife. "You can have a credit card when you start earning your own money and can afford to have one", Rachel had mandated. 'Like mother, like daughter', bitterly Rhea thought about her mother and grandmother. She snorted out loud

Her train of thought got back on track to memory-ville. She fondly recollected one of her visits to nana when she had been a little child. It was around Easter. Nana had given her a chocolate bunny with beautiful shiny wrapping. But one of the bunny's long ears had turned green with fungus. Rhea had simply snapped the infected ear off and enjoyed the rest of the bunny which had been made of the finest, silkiest Swiss chocolate. 'I wonder for how long Nana must have hidden that delicious bunny in her wardrobe, she smiled to herself. Then she shuddered as she had a chilling thought, 'how am I ever going to get through the summer!'

It was almost 9.30 AM when Rhea arrived at her grandmother's house. She had enjoyed the scenic car ride from the airport to the quaint little interior village. The fields were still green and held little pools of water which were speckled with white lotuses at this time of the year. Rhea directed the taxi to the quaint house that belonged to her grandmother. Nana was waiting on her balcony to greet Rhea. The old lady was nearing seventy but was still as agile and sprightly as ever. After all, she lived independently and had never accepted any money from her children.

She gave Rhea a warm hug and marveled at the deep mahogany highlights in Rhea's hair. The breakfast that she had laid out for Rhea was still warm – a cheese omelet with a side of butter and crispy pao. A cup of her special brew of tea sat steaming next to the plate of food. It was Nana's special blend of rose and Darjeeling tea. To Rhea, it tasted best milky and sweet. No matter how much she tried, Rachel could never replicate its marvelously satisfying flavour.

After breakfast, Nana led Rhea to the small bedroom adjoining hers. It was cosy and bright, with a large window that overlooked the garden. It contained a single bed, a narrow dresser, a wall cupboard and a few shelves on the wall bearing old books. Nana had made up the bed with fresh linen. The large colourful checked print of the bed cover suited the quaint, spotlessly clean room to perfection. Rhea expected nothing less. She knew very well that Nana was almost obsessive when it came to cleanliness and took to sweeping the whole house herself twice a day. Perhaps that was the secret to her physical health. Nana left Rhea to unpack and rest. She had decided to cook Rhea's favourite prawn curry for lunch and there was a lot to do in the kitchen.

Rhea did not waste any time getting started. She unpacked her clothes into the tiny old wall cupboard and hung up her dresses with hangers made of twisted wire. She carefully emptied her vanity case and set out all its contents neatly on the antique dresser. Then, just for fun, she decided to line up all her little bottles of nail polish on the window sill. She moved her head from side to side admiring how the sunlight lit up the glittery colours in the bottles. She quickly snapped a photo of her little exhibit and posted it on her social media to signal the commencement of her vacation. She changed into a comfortable pair of shorts and a T-shirt and slumped down on her bed. 'Now what?' she thought to herself. Before she knew it, she'd dozed off and woke up only a couple of hours later to the mouthwatering aroma of prawn curry and fish recheado.

Lunch with Nana was delicious and quiet. Nana was known as the best cook in the family and the tantalizing meal reminded her why. Nana enjoyed watching her relish her meal. When she had finished, she asked Rhea about her parents, her exams and all the expected topics of conversation. Rhea loved the food so much that she really did not mind humouring her Nana. She helped Nana clear the table and wash up and then slumped in front of the TV. She was relieved that Nana still had her cable connection. She had just flipped onto a popular music channel when Nana came in and said, "Rhea,

I need your help tomorrow. Can you come along for the paddeponn?"

"Sure Nana," Rhea replied a little intrigued. She had never been on a plucking trip or paddeponn before and she had nothing better to do anyway.

They left the house quite early the next morning so that all of the coconut trees on Nana's property could be plucked before the heat of noon. Rhea had dressed comfortably and shadowed her Nana. She watched intently as the 'padayee' or coconut plucker deftly rode up the slender trunks of the coconut trees. There were grooves etched out in the trunks of the trees to allow for a steady grip. In addition, the pluckers used a loop of rope around their ankles or wrists to scale it up in swift coordinated movements. Once they reached the top, they quickly relieved the tree of bunches of coconuts which were ready to be plucked, sagging palm leaves and even a few tender coconuts. These they carefully dropped in safe spots, to keep the workers below out of harm's way.

It seemed that those below knew exactly where to stand and when the plucker was done, for they quickly assembled to collect the coconuts in large bamboo-woven baskets. Rhea watched in amazement as men and women bent their knees slightly to receive baskets laden with coconuts on their heads cushioned only by coiled-up strips of cloth. The coconut leaves were stacked neatly and dragged away. These would be woven into mat-like structures which would be used to reinforce exposed walls or roofs. The coconuts were carried off to a storeroom adjoining the side of Nana's house. All the while, amidst the flurry of activity, Nana supervised and provided an instruction or two. The workers seemed to be well aware of the routine.

"Arre Sai!" Nana's cheerful greeting caught Rhea's attention. She turned around to watch a wiry young man, about the same age as her, dressed casually in smart jeans and a t-shirt stride towards them. He wore a wide grin that stretched from ear to ear. It took a second, but Rhea finally recognized the young man who had once been a friend when they were children. Sai lived in a small township not very far away but occasionally dropped by to visit his grandmother who was Nana's munkar. Rhea remembered that she knew Sai's grandmother as well. As a child, she fondly referred to her as Sai Aiee (Sai's mother). When finally faced with each other, Sai and Rhea shyly exchanged hellos and talked to each other for a while. Sai was pursuing his second year of mechanical engineering at the state engineering college and was presently on study leave. Rhea was pleasantly surprised that this young man from such humble roots was now in a professional college. She felt herself blushing and prayed that it wasn't too obvious.

When Rhea and Nana got back home, Rhea asked Nana about Sai and Nana was full of praise and admiration for the hard-working young man. She said that he had the determination and ambition to make something of his life. "Can his family afford to pay for his education?" Rhea inquired. "Oh, it's not much really. Being a government college, the fees are reasonable, but the quality of education is very good," Nana stated with confidence. The certainty in Nana's voice piqued Rhea's curiosity and she managed to get Nana to reveal that she was partially sponsoring Sai's education. "But don't tell your mama or your aunts!" Nana cautioned, "They won't understand." Rhea was taken aback. Was this the same penny-pinching amarenta that her mother always spoke about? Maybe she was not. She had noticed how at the end of the plucking trip, Nana had given away a lot of the coconuts to not only the workers but also poor families in the neighbourhood.

A few days later, Nana decided to tackle the mammoth task of cleaning her massive wooden wardrobe. It had been part of her trousseau and was one of her most prized possessions. It towered above her at over 6 feet in height and was as wide as it was deep. She had been staving off the herculean task, but Rhea's presence gave her the assurance she needed to see it through. They set about it together and started soon after a hearty breakfast.

Rhea set two large mats on the floor and confronted the wooden giant with her hands on her hips. At a petite 5'4" she had to look up at it. Nana produced a bunch of old keys from her dresser drawer. The lock of the wardrobe opened with a sharp click. It had double doors, with two additional panels on either side. These had to be opened separately by unlatching an internal lock. Nana opened them wide and exposed the belly of the beast. A pleasant aroma of mothballs mixed in with some kind of floral perfume wafted out. Slowly, the duo began the process of emptying shelves. Nana would hand over armfuls of clothes and stuffed plastic bags to Rhea, who would gently lay them out on the floor mats. She tried to maintain some kind of order so that she would know which shelf these would need to go back to. Next, they tackled the clothes that hung from hangers, which Rhea laid neatly on Nana's bed.

There were dresses in vivid colours, bold prints and in sizes that Rhea could not imagine her Nana in. The topmost shelves were out of reach, so Rhea used a stool and handed down the contents to Nana. Completely disemboweling the beast took a good thirty minutes, but that was just the easy part. Next, they wiped down the insides of the beast and changed the old yellowing newspaper that lined its shelves. Rhea looked at the dates on the old newspapers and gasped. These were from twenty years ago. She folded them up carefully and set them aside, it would make for interesting reading later on.

Once they had relined the empty shelves with fresh newspaper and strategically placed moth balls, they needed to sort through the contents of its belly. Nana parked herself on a chair while Rhea settled on the floor mats. They went through heaps and piles of things. Rhea was astonished to realize just how much of a hoarder Nana was. There were clothes from decades before that had not seen the light of day, for just as long. There were plastic bags of remnants of dress materials, tins of canned food, much of it expired, medicines, old photo albums, handbags and shoes of peeling leather, old cookbooks and women's magazines.

"Nana, we need to get rid of the things that are spoilt and keep aside the things that you don't use. Maybe we can donate it to charity." Rhea said firmly. Nana looked disheartened at the piles of things around her. It was obvious that she was reluctant to get rid of anything. "What if I need any of this someday?" she asked. Rhea knew that she had a difficult task ahead of her. She opted for the patient approach and gently prodded her grandmother to agree to get rid of a lot of items. Much of it, would be donated to charity. This was probably what eased Nana's burden and convinced her. Rhea sorted through everything, checking with Nana about every single thing. It took a long time and several breaks, but ultimately they were done. They had both worked relentlessly throughout the day and now it was almost evening. The wardrobe was neatly stacked and relieved of much of its baggage. The beast seemed to be less daunting, now that it had been tamed by the two daring women.

Just before closing the doors of the wardrobe, Nana surprised Rhea with a final request. She handed her a plastic bag and explained that it contained a dress and other items of clothing which were to be used for her funeral. Rhea solemnly nodded her acquiescence. She glanced at the items in the bag, before watching Nana neatly stack the bag on a shelf.

"What are we going to do with all of this?" Nana gestured to the pile of clothes on the floor mat.

"We'll donate everything that is in good condition to charity," Rhea assured her.

"Nana, there are so many things that have never been used. Why did you just keep them in the wardrobe?" Rhea asked.

"It's an old habit, Rhea," Nana began to explain, "You may not understand this, but in the old days we hardly had any money. It's not like it is now. Your grandfather had a modest salary and it was really up to me to make ends meet. We made a little money by selling the coconuts, coconut oil and other things that we got from our property. So I had to be careful with money and things and ration them carefully. It was the same when I was growing up."

Rhea carefully listened to Nana's story. She might not have been able to fully appreciate her grandparents' situation, but she felt that she had at least begun to understand their life. It had been simplicity in its true sense. Now, there were opportunities to make money and spend it, but life had become equally complicated, materialistic, unforgiving and competitive.

Rhea's new found understanding of her grandmother changed the way she regarded her vacation. She enjoyed immersing herself in new experiences. She delighted in the simple things, things that she would not be able to do in the big city like watering the plants in Nana's garden, and taking long walks through the paddy fields, and going to the Saturday bazaar with Nana. The bazaar could not have been more different than the mall. There were people there selling everything from vegetables to grinding stones. 'Genuine' was the best way to describe it. On Sunday mornings, she walked with Nana to church and relished the proud way in which Nana would introduce her to her friends.

Rhea's holiday would soon come to an end. If it had taught her anything, it had been the value of a simple life. Maybe her mother had been right in making her spend the summer with Nana. She would never admit it to her, thought. She would keep it to herself for as long as she could.

6

The Long Engagement

Bryan

I first saw her at church. She looked like an angel and sang in the choir – an angelic face with a voice to match. She captivated me immediately. Like a fool, I must have stared at her throughout the mass. I wonder if she noticed. Mummy certainly did and teased me about it, all the way home. She didn't stop at that of course. Once home, she told dad. How embarrassing! The fact was that I was of marriageable age and my parents had been looking for a girl for me. They never talked to me about it, but I know them well enough. I was back in Goa for a long overdue holiday having spent the last three years of my life in Dubai. I was a civil engineer and held a good position in an established construction firm. I was well-liked by my superiors and was earning very well. The time was ripe to settle down. I'd always wanted a gorgeous wife, one whose face would light up my day. For the first time, that day in church, I felt like I had finally seen someone who met all of my expectations.

My father has been delighted to join my mother in her relentless teasing of me. I tried to ignore them all along, but at dinner, I decided to put us all out of our misery.

"Alright, fine! Yes, I am interested in that girl. Are you happy now?" I asked in surrender. They both giggled like teenagers. "Who is she?" I prodded. "Her name is Renee," my mother offered. "She is our current reigning village beauty. I know that there are several young men vying for her. If you want her, we need to act fast and speak to her family", she said. I must have seemed pensive for she squeezed my arm and added, "Those other fellows are no match for you, my son! But still, let's not waste any time. What do you say?" she asked me in excitement.

The prospect of someone new in my life made me blush and I said yes. I had been in a couple of relationships before. But both were never meant to be anything serious. The first was with a girl from my batch in engineering college. We went steady for about two years but gradually drifted apart after graduating. The other had been during my first year in Dubai. She was pretty and foreign. We had some good times, but my parents would have never approved of her. I had been wise to call it off when I did. Would the lovely Renee be my third? I'd always considered number three to be my lucky number. I was excited and could barely sleep that night.

Mummy was true to her word. She did not waste any time in making enquiries and then approaching Renee's parents. She reported back to me as soon as she did. Renee had a spotless reputation. There were supposedly no boyfriends that anyone knew of. She was the youngest of three sisters, the eldest of whom was engaged to be married soon. Her parents had only one condition – they wanted a long engagement because they wanted Renee's two elder sisters to wed first. In addition, they wanted Renee who was just in her second year of college, to graduate before getting married. A long engagement was just fine by me! It would give us the time that we needed to get to know each other and also help me prepare for marriage, both mentally and otherwise. It was the perfect situation!

Renee and I had our first meeting at her family home in the presence of both our parents. She was far lovelier than I remembered and that thrilled me to no end. As expected, the meeting was very formal and awkward with barely a few words exchanged between us. But I got the feeling that she liked me. I would make certain that all of our meetings in the future would be held as privately as possible.

And so, we had our very first real conversation at a coffee shop. She wore a pretty floral dress that accentuated her great figure. She was nice and warm and easy to talk to. She didn't have any plans for her future and was more of a 'go-with-the-flow' type of person which suited me just fine.

We went on dates every day for almost a month. I made it a point to always show up with flowers or a gift. I knew that it never failed to delight her. She was conservative and I never pushed it beyond the point of holding hands or a chaste kiss on the cheek. I'd decided to take it slow. She was too precious to lose. We were engaged a month after our first formal meeting, which was just a week before I left. Mummy wanted the ring to be a family heirloom, but I wanted to buy Renee a ring that reflected me and so I did. She loved it and before I left, I French-kissed her to my heart's content.

Renee

I can't believe how fast things happened. I was introduced to Bryan one day and in no time at all, I was engaged to him! My parents were thrilled with the match. He met all their criteria. He was young, good-looking, had a good job and came from a good family. I'd never seen them happier, and their happiness pleased me to no end. I liked Bryan too. He was tall, attractive, and very nice to speak to. He was serious about our relationship, and he was willing to give me the time that I needed to get to know him better and become comfortable with the idea of starting a life together. He gave me a really expensive flashy ring. I like small pretty things. But I can't blame him for not knowing my taste in jewellery. After all, we had barely known each other for a month. Just before he left, he kissed me passionately. I was surprised by how much I enjoyed it. It meant that I was invested and willing to make this work. It was a first for me in so many respects. I had never been in a romantic relationship before this. My friends told me that I was too prudish, and they were right. It was the way in which I had been raised.

Bryan went back to work. He would be gone for a year and visit again the following Christmas. After he left, we made it a point to speak every day through video calls. Our phone calls went on for almost an hour and we spoke about everything and anything that we could think of. I found myself thinking about him every day and eagerly looking forward to our late evening calls. Everything was going on beautifully, until it wasn't.

It started as a patch of pink on my left elbow as if my natural skin colour had dissipated and exposed the delicate layer beneath it. When my mother saw it, she was immediately concerned and took me to a dermatologist. The diagnosis was a nightmare, vitiligo – a condition where the skin gradually loses its natural pigmentation, to reveal the pale skin beneath. However, the process is painfully slow and long. I had seen people with vitiligo before with their faces covered with odd-looking pale patches. I couldn't imagine that happening to me. I had always been pretty. I liked the fact that I could draw people's attention when I entered a room. My sisters were also very pretty. However, I would like to think that we were not very vain.

My mother went into a panic when she heard what the doctor had to say. No amount of reassurance that he offered could ease her mind. Yet I was strangely calm. Reality hadn't sunk in at that point. It hit me immediately after we got home. Mama was more worried about Bryan, about his reaction to this new development, about the future of our arranged marriage, about my future. I was aware that it had been my looks that had attracted him to me. We had been strangers before we met. If he broke it off with me, what prospects would a girl with vitiligo have?

There was an unyielding silence in our home that night. I could feel the strain and the tension. By the next morning, my mother had finally collected herself. She broke her silence and sat me down for a conversation. She surprised me that day. "Say nothing," she advised, "we'll see what happens when the time comes." I was speechless. I thought that it was madness, and what's worse, it was a lie! Two years was a long time. I was terrified of what the vitiligo might do to me during that time. How could I deceive Bryan like this? How could mama even ask me to? His parents lived in the same village. They would come to know sooner or later. But no matter how much I tried to convince my mother that we needed to disclose my condition, she simply wouldn't budge. I looked at my father in despair. It was obvious that he was uncomfortable with this too. But in our house, it was my mother who always had the final say in things.

Awkwardness crept into my conversations with Bryan. I made every excuse to avoid video calls. I just felt guilty and immensely uncomfortable to face him, instead I posted a lot of photographs of everyday life on social media. He seemed to accept this shift in our method of communication. There was still nothing wrong with my face. I closely studied it in the mirror every day and for about eight months, it was fine. Until it was not. About two months before Bryan was set to visit Goa, the first telltale sign of vitiligo made its appearance on my face – a speck of pink at the corner of my mouth. It seemed to grow a bit every time I saw myself in the mirror. I began studying my face more and more often. I was filled with despair until I stressed myself out to the point of admitting defeat. What was the point of all of this? There was no way I could fight this. I just had to accept things. Bryan and I had grown very close. I had accepted him as my partner for life. I was certain that he felt the same way about me. I longed to see him in person again, no matter the cost. I had also made up my mind to tell him the truth about my condition, even if it meant going against my mother.

Bryan

I got back home exactly a week before Christmas. I couldn't wait to see Renee. The sweet anticipation of what was to come had kept me in a euphoric mood for several days before I landed home. I longed to look at her, touch her and hold her to my heart's content. I was certain that she would be just as excited. I had already made plans to meet her on the very same day that I arrived. I had made dinner reservations at a promising new restaurant. When I picked her up that evening, she looked as lovely as ever. She wore a pale-coloured flowing dress which hugged her body in all the right places. Her hair was shoulder-length and she had left it loose. We had been speaking every day for almost a year, but she seemed so demure and shy. I couldn't help but keep staring at her as I struggled to concentrate on driving. Finally, I reached for her hand and clasped it in mine. It was just as petite and soft as I remembered it to be. It was a shame that I had to let it go momentarily every time I needed to shift gears.

The lighting at the restaurant was dim and romantic. Renee was still so shy and for some reason felt a little distant. She kept glancing at me and then away. I tried to find out what was wrong, but she said she was fine. I plied her with a glass of wine and finally saw her relax. We began speaking freely again. I reminded her that we would be married in another year. She immediately perked up at the mere mention of wedding arrangements. I encouraged her to speak about her ideas for the wedding theme, the venue, and the reception. To be truthful, I was not really listening, but the melody of her gentle voice had me captivated. We made plans for our next date. She suggested a restaurant that she wanted to try. I dropped her home, and we share a deep much-awaited kiss before she left. What a night!

I had been granted leave for just two weeks and every time we met, it was always at dinner. We had a ball of a time at the New Year's Eve dance. I had to leave a couple of days later. I wanted to spend more time with her on New Year's Day, so I surprised her with a picnic. I got mummy to pack us a picnic lunch and made my way to her house. She seemed quite taken aback but did not waste any time in joining me. I got the feeling that her parents may not have been thrilled with my showing up unexpectedly on New Year's Day. But I stepped into their home and offered them my best wishes along with my brightest smile and off we went.

Renee wore fitting jeans and a flowing top and looked enticing. I had picked out one of the more secluded beaches down south. We set out a mat with the picnic lunch and lazed about on the soft white sand. It was there in the bright sunlight that I noticed it – a speck of discolouration at the corner of her mouth. I asked her about it and she froze. Then she let out a deep sigh and told me the truth. She had vitiligo. I was not very familiar with the word, so she explained it to me in scientific terms. It was a gradual erosion of skin pigmentation' "Oh, okay," I said not grasping the gravity of the situation. But it was a detail that I could not forget and as soon as I got home, I looked it up online. I was shocked by the pictures that flashed on my screen. I couldn't imagine my lovely Renee looking like those people. But it was an inevitability that I could not shake. 'Oh, God! What do I do?' I thought anxiously. I did not speak a word of it to anyone else and left as planned a couple of days later.

In the weeks that followed I was tormented. Could I live with someone who had full-blown vitiligo? Yet, if I broke off our engagement now, she would hail me as a villain for the rest of her life. But the logical part of my brain told me that the sooner I ended it the better it would be. After all, she was very young and could find someone else, someone more accepting of her condition. Thank God for the long engagement! Or I might have been married by now without the slightest idea. I was not the guilty party here; she had concealed the truth from me. She should have told me about the disease as soon as she found out about it. But she hadn't on purpose. Yes indeed! She had deceived me. This was all the justification that I needed to end the engagement.

I spoke to my parents first. They were upset with my decision until they heard my explanation. Then, they were angry that Renee's skin disease had not been revealed to us. They told me to proceed with what I had to do. The next step was the hard part – actually breaking up with her. Luckily ours was a long-distance relationship. I planned a telephone conversation over the weekend. "I am sorry, Renee," I said, "I don't think that things will work out between us. We should call off the engagement."

"Is it because of the vitiligo?" she asked, getting directly to the point which was so unlike her.

"I am sorry", was all I said before ending the phone call. My parents would take care of the rest.

Renee

I was numb after Bryan broke up with me. But a part of me had been expecting it. I did not doubt that it was because of the vitiligo. I just lay silently in my bed that night and stared at the sparkling ring that he had placed on my finger. The next morning, I told my parents of what had transpired the night before. My mother grew hysterical. She stormed into the kitchen. For a long while, all we could hear was the loud deliberate clatter of pots and pans. My father remained his calm and sensible self. He clasped my arm and told me that it would be fine. Everything would be fine.

The very next day Bryan's parents visited our home. They came to return the ring I had given Bryan and formally break off the engagement. I wondered how Bryan got the ring back to them so soon. He must have sent it back by a super express courier service, I told myself, glad that I could find some humour in such a pathetic situation. They were impolite to the point of being hostile. They demanded to know why they had not been informed about my 'skin disease'. They accused us of deception. My mother burst into tears. My father apologized to them in his usual calm and dignified manner and politely bade them goodbye. I took Bryan's sparkly ring off my finger and offered it to Bryan's mother. "Keep it", she dismissed me haughtily and walked out. I couldn't understand why they would leave behind a valuable ring. Maybe they thought it was bad luck to take it back, I pondered. I was already too tired to make any sense of the situation.

Thank God, that's the end of it, I told myself. But I was sadly mistaken. Nasty gossip began making the rounds of our tiny village about how I had this horrid skin disease and that we had deliberately deceived Bryan and his family. I had been sad and ashamed until then. I knew that it had been wrong of me to not tell Bryan sooner. But now I was angry at Bryan and his parents. I'd thought that they had some class, but I was clearly mistaken. Why else would they have gone around defaming my family? My oldest sister was about to get married. I wished that they had shown some consideration towards her. The gossip took the biggest toll on my mother. I would sometimes catch her looking at me with such pity as if to say, 'and who will marry you now?' I had to stay strong. I kept repeating to myself,

"This too shall pass. This too shall pass." I had a giant patch of discolouration on my heart, and it was not caused by the vitiligo.

Strangely, the realization that I was not desirable anymore lit a fire in me. I would need to fend for myself. I did not want to be the object of anyone's pity or charity. I had to become someone formidable. I had never held any ambitions before. All that had changed overnight. Then I thought, what could be more formidable than the law?

Eight Years later

Renee

I seldom looked myself in the eye in the mirror. But whenever I did, the person that stared back at me was no longer a sweet-faced, naive girl. The woman staring back at me bore a face streaked with the marks of vitiligo, a mind sharpened by practice and purpose, and a heart toughened by sorrow and distrust. I had accomplished what I had set out to do. Corporate law was my forte. I had given up any semblance of a normal personal or social life to rise through the ranks of a prestigious law firm in Mumbai. I had meticulously earned my reputation as a consummate professional, absolutely capable, but impersonal and aloof. When people stared at my face, which they often did, especially if they'd just met me, I leveled their gaze with a steely one of my own until they shriveled back in awkwardness.

I was a rising star at my law firm. My colleagues valued me for my ability and my passion and not my face. I was handsomely paid, fiercely independent, and owned an apartment and car. I groomed myself to look the part – great clothes and accessories, perfect hair. I never tried to cover the blemishes on my face with make-up, but subtly accentuated my eyes and mouth. I worked out every day in the office gym, ate healthy food and tried to look after my health as best as I could. I had learnt the value of good health the hard way.

Back home, my two older sisters were married with beautiful children. My parents were well cared for and adored by their grandchildren. But I knew that they were still worried about my being alone. I had assured them time and time again, but they still wished that I would marry and have someone to call my own. I, on the other hand, had abandoned that aspiration a long time ago. I knew for a fact that a couple of colleagues at work were attracted to me. But I always maintained my distance and never displayed any vulnerability unless it was needed to achieve an objective.

Bryan

I was back at home again on vacation. The place had changed quite a lot but so had I. Fortunately, my parents were still in good health. They looked after me as if I was still a kid, even though I was a grown man fast approaching forty, whose life had come full circle. I was newly single and looking to start anew. Perhaps this was what had prompted me to come back home for a bit. I needed to rejuvenate. My divorce had come through a month ago. It had been hell. I had lost half of my money, my peace of mind and my pride to my ex-wife. Damn her!

I had been besotted by her the moment we met. She had been the woman of my dreams, beautiful and poised. She was a model with a flamboyant lifestyle and a myriad of suitors. But she chose me. I had been flattered beyond belief. After we married, I was not comfortable with her modelling career. So, she gave it up, but not her lavish tastes. She spent money like water. We argued about it endlessly. She was always quick to point out that this would never have been an issue had she continued modelling, so essentially it was all my fault. I don't know why or how we managed to stick it out for four years. We did not have any children. In hindsight, we did love each other in the beginning, but the money problems were just too large to overcome. My parents had been very disappointed. But they remained supportive of me. They wanted me to just forget about the episode and move on with my life.

I was just whiling away my time back home when the unthinkable happened. I saw Renee again. I had been told in passing that she was now a hot-shot lawyer and working at a firm in Mumbai. I remember feeling surprised that someone as demure and laid-back as Renee had become a lawyer. I was at a friend's wedding, and she was the last person from my past that I had expected to see. Only this Renee was no longer the shy girl I once knew. The woman before my eyes, stood tall and proud, in expensive heels, an expensive suit, and immaculately styled short hair. I watched her from a distance. Her face bore the discolouration of vitiligo. But she exuded a new confidence that attracted me to her all over again. In a few years, the last dark patches of pigment on her face would be gone and she would be an absolute stunner. I made discrete inquiries with friends and learnt that she was hugely successful and still single. I came back home and found that I could not stop thinking about her. I wondered how much she had changed. I wondered if I still stood a chance with her. I had to find out or I would regret it forever.

The next morning, I spoke to mummy. She was dumbfounded. She told me that I was mad to even think about it. It would be too shameful to go back to that family after we had rejected their daughter once before. What would people say? She had very valid reasons for not wanting to do this. But I begged her and kept at it for a couple of days until she gave in. I know that I was being an absolute coward, hiding behind my mother. But I couldn't help myself. I had to see this through.

Renee

I had just finished my second cup of coffee while going through the financial section of the morning paper. My brief visit home was nearing its end. I would fly back to my world tomorrow. My father sat with me in companionable silence. My mother came back from church in a mad frenzy. My father and I both looked up at her alarmed. She struggled to catch her breath and then began speaking rapidly. It took her a few moments to begin making any sense. At church, she had been approached by Bryan's mother with a proposal of marriage no less! "His mother told me that they were sorry for what happened the last time. She says that Bryan has changed so much. He is very interested in getting back together with you!" my mother fumbled. She had been so confounded upon hearing Bryan's mother, that she had been rendered speechless and unable to answer the woman. She had just high-tailed out of there.

"You should have slapped her face!" my father snarled with his teeth clenched. It was so unlike him. "Those scoundrels!" he muttered, "How dare they? After all that they have done?"

My mother looked at me helplessly. I was shocked to find that her eyes were hopeful. I felt so sorry for her. "What shall I tell her?" she asked me timidly. It was so unlike her. I put a reassuring hand on her shoulder and said to her gently, "You don't have to worry about anything. I will take care of it." I met my father's worried gaze with confidence so that he could be at ease as well.

I contacted Bryan directly. I could tell that he was taken aback. "Let's have dinner", I said nonchalantly. I named the time and place and he eagerly agreed. My parents wondered what I was up to. But thankfully, they left me to my own devices. I arrived at the restaurant sometime before Bryan was expected and took a seat facing the entrance. I needed to size him up. I knew all about his recent past, his recent divorce. I was infuriated by the nerve of him, but at the same time, I felt a strange curiosity.

He walked in on time. He had aged and gained some weight. It was especially evident on his face and waist. He smiled broadly when he spotted me as if we were long-lost friends. I smiled back at him and indicated that he could take the seat next to me. "Hello Renee, how have you been?" he grinned as he sat down. "I am fine. How have you been?" I offered. We exchanged pleasantries and made small talk.

"I am so sorry about what happened between us the last time," he finally said, "I was wondering if you would give our relationship one more chance."

I noted that he had not admitted to any wrongdoing on his part. "But why now, after all these years?" I asked him. He fumbled for an answer and just muttered something about second chances. He was hiding something. I decided to press on, "I know that you were drawn to me for the way I looked. As you can see, I no longer look like the girl you once liked. And yet you say you are interested in marrying me. I don't think I am good enough to be your wife", I said.

"Oh no Renee, please don't say that. You are a wonderful person," he gallantly rose to my rescue with his praises. "And look at you now, you are successful and, in a few years, when the pigmentation from your face clears, you will be absolutely beautiful again!"

And there it was! I thought to myself – evidence that Bryan had long changed at all. He was still as shallow as he had been. My face revealed nothing. I had been told that my poker face was impenetrable. Calmly I reached for my bag. I looked Bryan in the eye and said calmly,

"I can tell you right now that my answer is and forever will be No." I pulled out the engagement ring that he had left me with and placed it on the empty plate before him. I had looked at it countless times over the last eight years. It had always goaded me to work harder. I didn't need it anymore. "Goodbye Bryan," I said as I stood up and walked out. He didn't bother to follow me. The waiter who had greeted us walked past me with a quizzical look on his face.

Outside, the night air was cool and clean. My heart felt light and free like it was finally ready to move on.

7

Pandemic Bird

'Rook..rook..rook', went on the bird. It was eerily silent for early evening. 'Rook rook rook', it went again. What was this strange-sounding bird? I wondered to myself. I had been here for more than a month now and had never heard the bird before. 'Here' was Goa. It had always been a dream of mine to come here. My mother's ancestry was Goan. She had been born and raised here but had seldom visited after she married my father against her parent's wishes. My maternal grandparents were long gone now, and my mother had never maintained any relations with her side of the family. I had been born and raised in Pune. My mother's homeland had acquired some kind of mystical quality in my mind, and it had become a cherished dream of mine to come here.

Finally, at the age of twenty-six, as a full-fledged software professional, I decided to take an extended work-vacation to Goa along with two of my closest work colleagues. We convinced our project manager to sanction a work-from-home arrangement for four weeks. We had undoubtedly earned it after successfully meeting an important project milestone with great success. As soon as he'd relented, we packed our bags and laptops and heartily moved into our newly rented digs. It had been my idea to rent a little house rather than a flat or service apartment. I had lived my whole life out of a compact two bedroom-hall-kitchen apartment. I wanted to experience the luxury of space. I would have preferred a quaint little house in a peaceful village, but my colleagues were adamant that they wanted to experience Goa's infamous nightlife.

We were indeed fortunate to be able to find a small house with a little compound around it, in the northern coastal belt that is otherwise teeming with hotels and buildings. The house stood adjacent to a large hotel but was part of a modest neighbourhood of other similar dwellings. It was the hotel that looked out of place in the little residential setting. Loud music emanated from its grounds well past 11 PM even on weekdays. This would not have been tolerated in my city. The lane around the hotel, that was the access to the residential area, was always choked with taxis and rental vehicles. It must have all been quite a headache for the locals. But the three of us were fully committed to our own little plan to be able to afford such considerations. We planned to work hard and party harder. We had even rented a couple of bikes to be able to move about with ease. Our parents had been concerned of course, but the fact that it was the three of us together had put their minds at ease. I, Anuradha was the older and presumably the wiser of the group. My colleagues Suman and Sunaina were siblings separated in age by only a year. They were a tad wilder than I was. We joined the company together soon after graduation and had become fast friends ever since.

Everything was going according to plan until Suman and Sunaina were called back home early due to the untimely demise of their grandmother. We still had a whole week to go before we were scheduled to return to the office. I was really sorry to leave prematurely so I decided to stick it out for the remaining week by myself. The sisters left on the eighteenth of March 2020 and exactly five days after that, India was in a state of complete lockdown due to the onset of the Covid19 pandemic. I was stranded! My parents called me in a state of panic. I assured them that I had everything under control. I felt confident that I could do this. I called my office and made arrangements. I informed the landlord. I thought that I was all set. Then reality began to sink in. I had limited food supplies and no way of getting any more. Water was not a problem, but we hadn't exactly been properly shopping for groceries. I had eggs, instant soups, coffee powder, milk powder, tea bags, instant noodles and microwaveable popcorn.

Suman had purchased a dozen mankurad mangoes at my urging, which she had thankfully left behind. They had ripened to perfection. Whenever I held one in my hand, it felt like holding a warm heart-alive, aromatic and radiant like the summer. 'Mankurad' mummy had told me was the king of all mangoes. I felt glad that I had instigated the purchase. I could not afford to have even one of my precious mangoes go bad, so I left out a couple that I would eat that day and of the rest, I scooped out every ounce of juicy flesh, packed it into tiffin boxes and put it into the freezer. From experience, I knew that the local supermarket did not deliver groceries to the house. We did successfully order pizza and take-out food from local restaurants though. But I had no idea about what still worked in this bizarre situation. However, I was unfazed. For the first time in my life, I would be living alone and truly tasting independence, although in the most trying circumstances. It would be an adventure for sure.

The first week was a concerto in silence. There were no people on the road, no cars or vehicles. The usually bustling and noisy hotel next door was dead silent. The television was the only source of sound in the little house. At times, I would just switch it off for a few minutes to absorb the silence which was a complete stranger to me. I would just close my eyes for a few minutes and enjoy hearing nothing. This was when I first heard the 'rook rook rook' of the unknown bird. It seemed to patrol the neighbourhood several times a day end emitted its sound on each of its rounds. Even in the dead of night, a slight flurry of wind, would startle it and prompt it to let out its high-pitched 'rook rook rook'. I was eager to catch a glimpse of this creature, this pandemic bird.

The general silence amplified the sounds of the human element of the actual neighbourhood. Just adjacent to my house and compound wall, lived a family ruled over by a loud matriarch. I would hear her barking orders at various family members at all hours of the day. In the late evening, the hum of prayer resonated from their house. I could tell that it was the rosary. My mother still recited it especially in times of stress even though she had married outside of her faith. When I had been a child, she'd taught me to recite prayers like the 'Our Father' and the 'Hail Mary', even though she did not practice Christianity anymore. I'd found the 'Our father' to be a comforting and soothing presence in my life. I took after my mother in my habit of reciting it in stressful situations, long journeys and the like.

I felt greatly comforted as I listened to the familiar intonation of the rosary that streamed into my little home from my neighbours, the D'souza family. The words were barely audible, but the rhythm reminded me of my childhood with my mother. At times the mellifluous flow of prayers would be rudely interrupted by the senior Mrs. De Souza barking orders at someone or something. Wow! That woman never stops, I shuddered, thinking of how unnerving it would be to live with someone like her in the house. I soon came to befriend the younger of Mrs. De Souza's two daughters-in-law while she was attempting to pluck guavas from the guava tree that leaned into my compound. Her name was Lisa, and she was this petite sweet woman whose husband worked in the merchant navy. He was barely home for most of the year. I admired her for her ability to live with such a formidable mother-in-law. We exchanged phone numbers and were soon into each other's social media. At the end of the first week, when my food supplies were dwindling, she surreptitiously slipped me a couple of biscuit packets and a tin of cheese over the compound wall. That sealed our friendship. Thereafter, she would call me often, just to talk and vent about her home life. I couldn't blame her, poor thing! I was glad that I could at least offer her a listening ear.

In the middle of the second week, salvation rolled in on four wheels. I was startled to see a small goods carrier moving through the neighbourhood. I came out into the balcony with a scarf tied around my face. I was surprised to find a handsome young man standing at my gate beside the goods carrier. He was dressed in casual clothes which were too smart for a mere driver of a goods carrier. My guard was up. He was not wearing a mask and waved to me amicably from a distance and introduced himself as 'Bruno'. He explained that he had obtained special permission to sell groceries to stranded families. I felt myself relaxing and feeling relieved. As I walked towards the gate, he quickly pulled out a surgical mask from his front pocket and masked himself. He told me that he would visit every week and so I bought sufficient groceries to last a little more than a week. He had a nice deep voice and spoke English perfectly well. He was obviously well-educated. I couldn't help but wonder what exactly his deal was. Thankfully my face was covered enough to hide my curious expression. He seemed curious about me himself and I exercised caution and told him the bare minimum – I was a tourist, just passing through. He pulled out a business card from his pocket and handed it to me. I had a look at it after he had driven away. He was in fact the proprietor of a local restaurant that was quite well-known for its seafood. The girls and I had always intended to eat there but never had the chance. Why would the owner of a successful restaurant be delivering groceries? I decided to ask him the next time he visited.

I could discern that Bruno's visit had provided much-needed relief to the entire neighbourhood. But I couldn't help but notice the forlorn figure of the old lady who lived directly across my house. Lisa had told me that she was known as Consao Aunty by everyone in the neighbourhood. She was a widow with no family who had lived alone for many years. She always wore pale-coloured cotton sarees. Her favourite pastime was sitting out on her balcony and watching the world go by. Lisa had told me that the neighbours often stopped by and made small talk with her. She wasn't the gossiping type, just a lonely old lady looking for a bit of conversation. Now that everyone was housebound, there was no one really to talk to her and she must have felt even lonelier.

In the evenings she would begin her vigil at about 5.00 PM, in wait for the podder on his trusted old bicycle. I had been fascinated by the age-old concept of the podder in Goa. The podder was essentially the bread-man who strapped a large cane basket to the back seat of his bicycle and sold his wares from door to door. He would announce his arrival with the help of a loud and comical horn that emitted a ponk ponk sound. Aunty Consao always bought the same thing every day, two poies, one for dinner and the other for breakfast. But now, the podder had not come by for days because of the lockdown. This had caused Aunty Consao a great deal of anxiety.

I had always greeted Consao aunty from across my gate. But that day I decided to take things a step further. I couldn't speak Konkani but could understand it well enough. "Hello Aunty", I greeted. As usual, she smiled and nodded at me. "How are you, aunty?" I asked. She replied in pristine Konkani and told me that she was worried that the podder hadn't come by for several days. She needed her poies because she did not eat rice at night and arthritis in her hands prevented her from kneading the dough to make chapathis. She had been sorely missing the podder and his poies. I offered to make her chappatis. She considered it for a while before graciously accepting. She said that she needed only two chappatis per day and said that she would pay me for them. Not wanting to offend her, I told her that she could pay me later. Would five rupees a chappati be enough? She inquired. I nodded that it was absolutely fine. And so, I could finally put to use the chappati-making skills that my mother had tried so hard to instill in me. I was more than happy to put Consao aunty's mind at ease. In the process, not only did I also make chappatis for myself and begin to have a wholesome dinner, but I also made another friend in the neighbourhood.

Late evenings were very quiet in the neighbourhood. I could hear the heavy tolling of the church bell as it chimed promptly at 7 PM every day. I set my work timings by it and shut down my laptop for the day. I had asked Lisa about it, and she'd told me that it signified that it was time for the Angelus to be recited. I'd been educated in a convent school and faintly remembered the prayer. This time of dusk became my favourite time of the day. I would let my balcony sit in darkness, while

I sunk into the cool cemented seat with a cup of hot tea and relish the light evening breeze. The air was clear and sweet. There was no traffic for miles on end, that had to be the main reason for it. The internet was full of articles and pictures of how the earth was coming back to life, thanks to the imposed lockdowns. It reminded me of the rook rook bird. As if on cue, 'rook rook rook', it called out to me. Unfortunately, I still hadn't caught sight of it and hoped that I would soon.

In the evenings, I spoke to my parents and friends while I sipped on my hot tea. Suman and Sunaina who had initially counted themselves lucky to have left before the lockdown, sorely missed our time together in the little house now. They lived with their parents in a two-bedroom flat. But it had so happened that their older brother, his wife and twin boys were also stranded with them, thanks to the lockdown. The boys were boisterous and noisy, the apartment was crowded, and temperaments were strained and on edge. Everyone was walking on eggshells, all of the time. They longed for the happy camaraderie, peace, and space that we had shared just a few weeks ago.

For a while, I followed the news and statistics and kept track of the number of infected Covid cases and deaths. But I began to get scared and depressed. And so, I just stopped. I would just let ignorance become my bliss. I would follow all the precautions, but it was pointless becoming paranoid. Movies made earlier about epidemics and diseases started becoming popular again. I figured that those who watched these again as reruns were just being gluttons for punishment. It was best to just stay away from all the negativity. It didn't mean that I did not appreciate the enormity of the situation. I just held it at arm's length for the sake of my mental well-being. I advised my parents to do the same.

All around me in the unfamiliar silence, I observed as my new neighbours went about their lives – the D'souzas and their shrill matriarch across my compound wall, the eerily silent hotel at the other end and the vigilant Consao aunty out in front. Now and then the old uncle from down the lane motored past my house on his noisy old scooter, fishing line in tow at the crack of dawn. Come rain or sunshine, he just couldn't quit his fishing habit or, so Consao aunty told me. His favourite spot was the bridge across the creek that ran through the village. Even at the height of the pandemic, no cop nor foe could deter the old man from his life's passion.

The next week Bruno rolled in with his vegetable carrier right on schedule. I had been expecting him and had placed an order beforehand. He waved at me from outside my gate. Although his face was covered in a mask, his eyes revealed that he was smiling. I smiled back from behind my mask and walked towards the gate. He had carefully placed two bags of groceries inside and shut the gate behind him. I handed him the money over the gate.

"I am sorry that I didn't catch your name the last time", he said. I could hear the smile in his voice.

"Anuradha, but everyone calls me Anu", I replied.

"Nice to meet you, Anu. I am.." he said.

"Bruno, I know", I completed his sentence for him. "You gave me your card the last time", I said by way of explanation. "How come a restaurant owner is out delivering groceries?" I asked.

"Well, the restaurant had to be shut and I needed to do something. This way I can continue paying my staff". He replied.

"Oh", I nodded, "Someday I will come to your restaurant", I smiled.

"You are always welcome", he smiled back. He nodded his goodbye politely before getting into his vehicle and driving away. I watched him for a while. I thought that he was quite handsome and then immediately chided myself at the thought. I was probably just getting the lonely pandemic blues.

'Rook rook rook', the mysterious bird called out as if to confirm my theory. I strained my neck trying to catch a glimpse of it but in vain. The sun felt warm and pleasant. Yet another beautiful day I thought to myself before heading in.

This unexpected routine became my life for the next few weeks. I was alone but never lonely. In the early morning, I took several laps around my compound. I worked steadily throughout the day and took several breaks on my balcony. It was a lucky coincidence perhaps, but the rook rook bird frequently accompanied me on my breaks. I shut down my laptop for the day at the angelus bell and settled with my hot cup of tea on the balcony to bid adieu to the dusk. I chatted with my parents and friends during this time. After that, I would quickly roll out a couple of chappatis for Consao aunty. Suman and Sunaina called me at least thrice a week just to talk, and so did Lisa from next door. I didn't mind my newfound status as an agony aunt. I felt good to be of some help to them.

Bruno came by with deliveries every week. Whether I could admit it to myself or not, I looked forward to his visits. We made small talk over my gate, safely six feet apart, clad in masks. I realized that he had never seen my face in person. I did not want to appear too forward and contact him directly for anything other than groceries. His presence always felt warm and comfortable. But in all likelihood, he was just being a good businessman and keeping all his customers engaged in the same manner. Perhaps someday our paths would cross again under better circumstances. For now, I would leave it at that.

It took weeks for the worst of the first wave to subside and India cautiously opened its internal borders. I was faced with the decision of going home or staying. Going home of course seemed like the most likely choice for someone like me, someone with elderly parents waiting for them. And so, one by one I said my goodbyes to Lisa over the compound wall, to Consao aunty who was ecstatic that the podder was back on his rounds and to Bruno.

"I am leaving, going back home," I told him. We were both silent for a moment.

"Have a safe journey home", he said softly, "I will re-open my restaurant once things settle down. I hope that you keep your word and visit then." He said.

The night before I left, my bags were packed and ready. I lay back in the darkness and listened for the rook rook bird. It did not disappoint. Consao aunty told me that the bird had always been around. It was just that the din of commerce and the daily grind prevented anyone from noticing it. I asked her if she had seen it and she replied that she had. She said that it looked like a small egret, dull brown in colour. It occurred to me that it took a pandemic to discover a bird that had always existed, just like it had taken a pandemic to discover a small part of me. The part that tied me to my mother's homeland and the people here, a few of whom I'd had the pleasure of meeting. I made a promise that night, that once this terrible tide subsided, I would return to Goa not as a mere tourist, but as a daughter looking to discover home.

8

The Three Curses

My Avozinha carried a nugget of disappointment within her heart from the time she was eighteen, till the day she died some forty-five years later. It was during the Portuguese rule in Goa, that she was married into affluence at the age of eighteen. But not for long. Mama tells the story well...

At the age of eighteen, Emilia was the oldest of a brood of seven children. Her mother had taken ill after the birth of the youngest son. Therefore at the tender age of fourteen, Emilia had taken on all of the household duties. Like a faithful daughter, she had cooked and cleaned, bathed her younger siblings, and taken care of her ailing mother for nearly four years. But in the back of her mind, she often wondered if life would just pass her by. Would she end up an old bitter spinster like her aunt Fatima next door, who had given up having a home of her own, while her siblings flew the nest one by one? She shuddered at the thought of becoming nothing more than the in-house nanny and maid to one of her brother's families. She would never speak of this though, as a well-brought-up daughter never would.

All these thoughts simmered in her mind, while upon the firewood stove, a cauldron of soup did the same.

"Emilia!" she heard her mother call from her room.

"Yes, Mai" she called back and quickly wiped off her hands. She went to her mother's side.

Her mother bade her to sit by her bedside.

"Bai," she said affectionately, "You are a young lady now and we have been looking for a good match for you."

Emilia was surprised, but pleasantly so. She had not known of her parent's plans and her heart was filled with gratitude and affection. She gazed at her mother expectantly, then withdrew her gaze and lowered it to the ground.

"We have found a good boy for you from a good family," her mother smiled. His mother is Portuguese and his father was a civil servant in the Portuguese administration. The family is very influential and very well-to-do..." her mother paused. Emilia was intrigued. She looked up and saw her mother smiling at her fondly.

"Bai", her mother continued, "They have a mansion, the most beautiful house in the village. I passed by it once when your aunty Nina got married. It's magnificent! Your aunty Nina told me that the walls inside are covered with blue murals from Macau with blue crystal chandeliers to match."

Mai smiled as if at a loss for words to continue her description of the palatial mansion. Emilia blushed. She could not believe her good fortune. Mai produced a black and white photo of a handsome young man with a fashionable pencil-thin mustache. His name was Thomas and he was ten years older than Emilia. Emilia bowed her head in silent consent. The age difference was quite the norm of the time. Mai smiled; her mind had now begun collating a long list of wedding preparations that needed to get done.

Emilia had three precious months at home before she would be married away. She would meet her bridegroom only at the altar, but that was the way of the world that she lived in. Her mind had become like a large pendulum that swung between nostalgia and euphoria. On the one hand, she would miss her parents, siblings, and extended family. On the other, she could not wait to become a "bhatkaan", mistress of a grand mansion and an estate. She would in no way miss the dreary life of caretaker and maid that she had been living for the past four years. Her second sister Maria would take care of things now.

A good life of luxury had always been a secret dream of hers. One she never thought would come true. But here it was! Within her grasp! The days flew by with her aunties and relatives making arrangements for her modest trousseau under the supervision of her mother. She felt like a queen for once. They waited on her hand and foot. "This is what the rest of my life will be like." she thought with great anticipation and gratitude.

On the day of the wedding, Emilia was woken up at 4 AM. She had been bathed in coconut milk the previous evening in a traditional ceremony called the "roce". It was a gathering of all her relatives and the entire neighbourhood. All of them had taken turns pouring handfuls of thick coconut milk on her and blessing her. The ceremony was meant to bless the bride and prepare her for her wedding. The thick coconut cream would soften and enliven her skin. The guests then took turns pouring tumblers of warm water over her all the while the people around her sang happy songs of love and dreams. Even early in the morning, she felt revitalized and excited.

Within the next couple of hours, she was decked in the modest finery that her family could afford. Her white wedding gown had been sewn by the village tailor. She wore a veil of fine lace that had been her mother's. The gloves she wore were hand crocheted by her aunts. Her wedding set was a delicate necklace and earrings of black platinum and marquisette stones. On her right arm, she wore six gold bangles intermittently spaced with green glass bangles that were meant to symbolize fertility, and a gold ring on her finger.

She wore new white shoes that had been sent for her by a kind relative from overseas. On her left hand, she wore a gold watch, a gift from her godfather. Her bouquet was made of simple white China roses and ferns that grew in her neighbour's garden. A 'consul' car had been hired to transport the bride and her parents to the church in the groom's village. Everyone else would follow them in the El Caminho.

The wedding party left the bride's residence at 8 AM in plenty of time to make the two-hour trip to the church for the nuptials at 11 AM. Emilia held her breadth as the white dome of her groom's church drew in sight. The whirlwind of emotions that had been raging in her head had died down to an eerie calm. The whole experience was surreal as she stepped out of the car with her parents and was received by the groom's family. Her father took her arm and led her to the door of the church, where at last she saw Thomas. His picture had done him justice, she thought in relief and her spirits were lifted once again. She floated through the wedding ceremony effortlessly. After the exchange of wedding vows and rings, Thomas lifted her veil. The two exchanged timid hasty glances with each other now that they were declared to be man and wife.

After church, she accompanied her husband in a different car to his home for the lunch that would be offered to all their guests. As she sat nervously beside him, excitement and pride swelled up inside her. She looked forward to seeing her new home, her new mansion, and the awe it would inspire in her family and their guests. They alighted from the car in what seemed like no time at all in front of a house that was decorated with colourful paper buntings. A 'mattao' had been set up in front of the house – a type of colourful cloth tent for the guests. Emilia looked at the house and felt disappointed for it was no bigger than her own parents' home.

The local brass band began playing an upbeat tune with gusto and Emilia's thoughts were scattered.

People dressed in their best attire were gathered on both sides of the tent to welcome the new couple with showers of flower petals and rice. The festivities had begun. Plates of pulao and xacuti and trays of drinks were hastily passed around – delicious food, but not food that was worthy of a mansion. Emilia was now afraid, confused, and close to tears. But she put on her bravest face and sturdiest smile. Perhaps there was a reasonable explanation for all of this. She would be in her mansion soon enough.

The festivities were over sooner than she would have liked. As evening fell, the guests began leaving in groups, her parents and siblings were the last to go. She held each of them tightly and cried as her heart melted at the sight of them leaving.

Soon the evening lamps were lit. Thomas and his Portuguese mother, Celeste led her into the house. Her spirits sank further as her worst fears were realized. The house was modest and just as big as her parent's house. But she held back her tears and her words bravely. After a light supper, Celeste led the new couple into their room. Emilia's trousseau and belongings had been delivered and neatly arranged the previous week, as was the custom.

No sooner than Emilia was alone in her room with Thomas, she broke down into sobs. Thomas tried to console her. He thought that it was understandable that she would miss her parents and siblings. But Emilia would not let him near her and continued to sob late into the night. An exasperated Thomas sat defeated across her on the bed. They both drifted to sleep on opposite sides of the bed still dressed in their finery. Emilia was the first to be awakened by the morning light. Thomas soon followed. By this time, she was calm enough to speak to him. Shyly she said, "I am sorry. I was upset last night."

He nodded silently. "Tell me, "She asked, "Is this your only home, for I was told that you had another."

At the time, Thomas did not realize the significance of that question.

"This is a rented house, Emilia." he said, "Our ancestral home is called Casa Anna, after my grandmother. But we do not live there anymore."

"Why?" Emilia almost cried out aloud. And Thomas told her.

Tia Delphine had been Thomas's aunt – his father's widowed older sister, who had chosen to live at her father's home along with her three daughters, after her husband's death. She was a tyrant who kept the household at Casa Anna running like clockwork. No one, not even Thomas's father would dare to go against her. Her main source of income came from her father's land, which included the annual rice paddy harvest and the monthly yield of precious coconuts. Casa Anna was the most beautiful mansion in the village, but Tia Delphine was not one to entertain annoying visitors. So these were few and far in between. Thomas and his parents took to visiting their friends outside the family home.

Tia Delphine had one aim in life. She wanted to see her three daughters, Anna, Agnela and Arlena, settled well. She was a different person around her daughters, warm and maternal. They were good girls – pretty, homely, and obedient. Anna had already been promised in marriage to a young man from a respectable family when the incident that changed their lives occurred.

Pedro was a tenant on their estate. It was said that he was the only one who had the nerve to talk back to Tia Delphine, as he disliked her intensely. The reason for this animosity which was quite mutual had been lost in history. Pedro worked on the coconut plantations on the estate diligently. He looked after coconut trees and coconut saplings as if they were his own children. He hated interference from Tia Delpine. He took great pride in the coconut saplings that he planted across the estate and nurtured them like they were his babies.

One monsoon, six months before Anna was to wed, he planted three of his best saplings near Casa Anna. Tia Delphine took strong objection to this. She felt that the saplings blocked her view of their neighbour's estate. One morning when the whole family was gathered for breakfast, she summoned Pedro and verbally shred him to pieces in the presence of the entire household, including the servants. Her insults got personal and vicious. Pedro went away in tears but refused to do away with his three precious saplings. In a rage at his insolence, Tia Delphine had all three saplings chopped down in Pedro's absence, that very day. When Pedro returned that evening, he marched to the house. Everyone knew that they were in for a massive showdown. But Pedro was eerily calm. The words he then spoke chilled everyone present in the room to the bone. He said to Tia Delphine, "Just like you killed my three saplings, so shall you lose each of your three daughters, one by one, in the order they were born."

After he left the house that evening, he disappeared and was never heard from again. News of what came to be known as the three curses spread through the village. But Tia Delphine would have none of it. She had a wedding to plan.

Anna was married with great pomp.

She died of pneumonia, two months thereafter.

Agnela died within the same year of a fever.

Tia Delphine clung to her precious youngest child, but could not prevail over death which came for Arlena in the following year. Tia Delphine was stricken with grief and was reduced to a shell of her former self. The darkness that descended over Casa Anna could not be lifted. The family came to believe that the house and all its treasures were cursed. They moved to a humble rented house down the road. Tia Delphine died there a couple of years later.

Casa Anna slowly died of neglect. Most of its treasures were stolen, and in the years that followed, the walls crumbled and succumbed to the elements. Thomas's family did nothing to stop this. They were glad to be rid of the curse.

It was in its ruined state that Emilia was given the grand tour of Casa Anna by Thomas, a week after her wedding. She could still see the blue murals from Macau on the walls that her mother had spoken about. She begged Thomas to salvage a few pieces of furniture that still stood, for the sparsely furnished house they now lived in. But he refused to touch the stuff.

Emilia's dreams of becoming the mistress of a grand mansion were thus shattered on the floors of Casa Anna.

I realized later in life that my avozinha never did get over this. It molded her into the person I knew and loved, for better or for worse.

9

Pescadora

Pamela stretched out her tired legs as she sipped from her cup of hot coffee. It was part of a routine that she had adhered to for almost thirty years, but her life tomorrow would be very different. The day had been her last day as a primary school teacher. She had turned sixty that same month and had retired after a career that had spanned almost three decades. The experience had been sentimental, to say the least. The school which was like a second home had hosted a generous retirement party for her. The ten-year-olds whom she taught had put a lot of effort into making colourful farewell cards. She had been showered by bouquets of flowers and had a steady stream of visitors many of whom were now seniors in the secondary school section. She had been emotional the whole day through. She had been fearful of this point in her life for a long time and the day had finally come.

Teaching had been her passion – the thing that had given her life a definitive purpose, a raison d'etre. She had wondered what she would do thereafter. Her son Neville, her only child was a grown-up married man with a young child of his own. Her husband Percy, who had retired some years ago, spent his time gardening, visiting friends and reading every possible newspaper available whilst consuming gallons of tea every day. He seemed to enjoy retirement, but she was sure that it simply wouldn't suit her. She had cultivated several options for community service and had offered her babysitting services to her son and daughter-in-law who lived a small distance away from her. But she was still wondering about what her next big step should be. She was well-known and well-respected in the village. She would need to put her time to good use and do something worthy of her stature as a teacher.

"Pamela, what are you thinking about?" Percy interrupted her thoughts, "You have been gloomy ever since you came home from school. You should be happy. You have finally retired. It's time to relax!" he said cheerfully.

Pamela shot him a look of irritation and sighed. Percy took the hint. He knew better than to offer her any more of his unsolicited advice.

"Oh, I have made reservations at Peter's Place tonight to celebrate your big day. Let's leave by 8, okay?" he said cautiously.

Pamela would have shot him down had he said something else. She loved Peter's place. The restaurant was actually named 'O Pescador' and was owned by Peter, a close family friend. They almost always referred to it as Peter's place. It was just by the sea and specialized in seafood. It was where they had dinner at least once a week, generally over weekends, for more than a couple of decades. Pamela offered a melodious 'Hmm hmm' to Peter's offer and he knew at once that she was happy with his evening plans.

Pamela loved the ambience at 'O Pescador'. The place was softly lit. Its walls were adorned with traditional hand-woven bamboo baskets and draped with fishing nets to give it a rustic look. The dark wooden floors were highly polished to add an air of sophistication. The male serving staff wore smartly outfitted black trousers and a shirt with a tropical print. The women wore black knee-length pencil skirts with blouses that bore the same tropical print as the men. They were mainly old-timers and were well aware of Pamela and Percy who were regulars and also good friends of the boss. The couple was always treated with the utmost reverence and courtesy. They always occupied the same table by the window that overlooked the sea.

There was a time when the restaurant windows were thrown open but over the years Peter had air-conditioned the place and the windows were now sealed shut with glass. Pamela always thought it a shame that this soundproofed the whole room and blocked out the wonderful sound of the ocean and the waves softly crashing on the shore.

Almost immediately upon the couple's arrival, the captain of the restaurant, a handsome young man, approached them and greeted them.

"Hello Polly", Pamela whispered loudly.

The young man blushed and replied, "Hello M'am."

He greeted her and Pamela beamed. Polly had been her student and was the son of one of her closest friends. She had known him since infancy and had watched him grow into a fine young man. He had been christened as Paulo but was fondly known as Polly to those closest to him. He had been a marvellous sportsman but not very good with books, much to his mother's dismay. She would have liked him to get into a professional line of work. But Pamela had always felt that Polly had indeed done very well for himself given his capabilities and strengths. She had always had a very big soft corner for him. She'd thought of him as her younger son, the second child she had always wanted but never had. Her only child, her son, Neville was a little older. He and his wife, Zelda and their little son Zayne lived in a town nearby. Neville had always said it was because of its proximity to his workplace and Zayne's school. But Pamela had always felt that it was Zelda who had instigated the move to put some distance between Pamela and her son. Pamela sighed at the thought. She had not realized it, but she and Zelda were a lot alike in temperament, both headstrong and direct. It was no wonder that they found it difficult to get along.

"M'am I am so sorry that I could not attend your retirement ceremony", Polly said, thus bringing Pamela out of her digressed thoughts.

"Oh Polly, don't worry about that. I know that I can always see you when I visit here, if not at your home", she reassured him.

He proceeded to take their orders for drinks and starters. Pamela usually never ordered for starters but she surprised Percy by ordering a portion of batter-fried prawns. He took it as a good sign that she was finally getting into retirement mode and grinned to himself.

"What are you smiling about?" she asked him pointedly after Polly had left the table.

"Oh nothing", he said nonchalantly, treading safely.

Pamela looked around the restaurant. The staff was at their stations, looking smart in their neat uniforms. Only Polly stood out in his crisp white formal shirt, narrow black tie, and dark trousers, to signify his status as captain of the serving staff.

"Don't you think that Polly ought to get married and settle down this year? He's already thirty-three", Pamela mused to Percy. "I should talk to Leena about it", Pamela said, referring to Polly's mother.

"Better not to interfere, my dear", Percy cautioned," I am sure that they know what they are doing."

"Hmm!" Pamela snorted.

'Why do I even bother?' Percy thought to himself with a soft sigh.

Pamela's gaze was drawn to a beautiful young woman, fair, slender, and graceful with oriental features. She was certainly a new staff member and stood smartly in her uniform on one side of the room.

"Oh, how pretty!" Pamela remarked causing Percy to instantly look in the same direction.

"Don't stare Percy!" she scolded him, "She must be new. I wonder what her name is." She raised her hand and beckoned the young lady to their table. The youngster immediately rushed to Pamela's side.

"How may I help you Madam?" she said softly in a lilting voice. Pamela just wanted an introduction and thus learnt that the young lady was called Glory and that she hailed from the northeastern part of India. She further engaged Glory in an easy-going conversation because she had always wanted to visit the beautiful region on holiday. The two made small talk for a couple of minutes after which Glory went back to her workstation.

Percy who had witnessed the whole conversation silently could tell that his wife was intrigued and had taken a liking to the pretty young woman. When their food arrived, the couple ate in companionable silence, quickly moving from one course to the next. Percy's eyes were glued to the large screen TV that was mounted on the adjacent wall. While Pamela spent her meal quietly observing all the other people in the restaurant, Percy absorbed the football match that unfolded on the big screen. It was no secret that he often planned their trips to the restaurant to coincide with the day on which a big match would be played. He rather enjoyed watching it on the big screen TV at 'O Pescador'.

By the middle of the main course, Pamela felt that she had made an interesting observation. Her beloved Polly kept staring in the direction of the lovely Glory. This tickled Pamela pink. She thought that perhaps Polly had finally fallen in love. Oh, how wonderful that would be! She said something to Percy, but he just grunted in response. She could tell that he was too immersed in the football match and decided that it was hopeless to speak to him then.

By the time that dessert had arrived, she was quite certain of her observations. She was delighted by the prospect of a new romance between her favourite pupil and the lovely new stranger.

On their way home from the restaurant, Pamela made a mention of her observations to Percy and remarked about how delighted she was. She went on to speculate whether Polly's mother Leena would approve of her son's fine choice.

"Pamela, please don't interfere," Percy cautioned her yet again.

"What? I haven't done anything. Honestly, it's pointless talking to you!" she erupted.

"I know you and you will do something," Percy gently scolded her; "All I am saying is just be certain of the facts first."

"Hmm!" Pamela huffed. It was a sign that Percy knew all too well. It meant that there would be no further discussion.

Pamela wished that Percy would give her more credit than he did. Of course, she would never utter a word until she was quite sure. And that she did. She carefully observed Polly and Glory during their visits to 'O Pescador' over the next few weeks. Polly gazed at her intently. Poor boy! She thought. He was much too shy to make the first move. He always had been. She couldn't bear to see him look so forlorn. She had to help him! She knew that Polly would never dare go against his mother, Leena's wishes. Leena would disapprove of him marrying outside their community and their faith. Ha! She was one to talk! Pamela mused. Leena had married outside her community and faith. Her marriage to Polly's father had been quite a scandal back in the day. She was considered an outcast in the neighbourhood and her own new home. Had it not been for Pamela's intervention, she would have continued to be one. She decided to swing this one in Polly's favour too.

During the next week, Pamela carefully contemplated what approach would best work for Polly's mother. She regarded and disregarded several options until she could not contain herself any longer. It was best to just be direct and get it over with. And thus, after five long days of internal deliberation, she set out to visit her good friend.

It was mid-morning and Leena was out in her garden spreading pieces of tamarind out on a bamboo mat. She saw Pamela approach and beamed up at her. Pamela waved and smiled back. The anxiety she had harboured left her and she felt that she had been nervous for no good reason at all. Leena greeted Pamela at her gate and escorted her into her home. Pamela gazed around and smiled in appreciation. Leena's home was immaculate. She had always taken great pride in maintaining it.

There was not a speck of dust in sight and the tables and cushions were dressed in linen which was finely embroidered by Leena. She took as much pride in maintaining herself as she did her home. Even at home, her hair was neatly coiffed, her clothes were neatly ironed, and she wore several pieces of gold jewellery.

The two long-time friends exchanged pleasantries and Leena quickly produced a cup of strong tea and a plate of doce just as Pamela has always liked. "Pamela, this is such a nice surprise. I can't remember the last time you visited me in the morning", Leena smiled. "Is retirement suiting you well?"

"Oh yes, it's fine," Pamela brushed it off before getting serious. "I was eager to talk to you about Polly."

Leena tensed, "Why? Is something wrong?"

"Not at all," Pamela reassured her, "I just wanted to know whether you had any luck with his marriage."

Leena sighed audibly and gave Pamela an exasperated look that said it all. Polly was already well into his thirties, but no matter how much or how hard she tried, he refused to consider marriage, refused to discuss it, or meet any of the girls she presented. Leena had implored Pamela to speak some sense into him and Pamela had indeed tried but Polly has just clammed up. Pamela had failed miserably.

"Leena, I may have some good news", Pamela offered. Leena immediately perked up, "Tell me, tell me", she demanded.

Pamela hesitated for a second, and then continued, "I think Polly may like someone at work. She has newly joined the restaurant and is very pretty."

"Really?" Leena heaved in excitement, "Do you know her? Do you know her family?"

"Well, no", Pamela tread with caution, "She is not Goan. I think that she is from one of the Northeastern states."

The light that had lit up Leena's face went dark, and she shook her head, "No Pamela, this won't do", she said firmly.

"Don't be so adamant about this, Leena", Pamela said gently. "Polly finally likes somebody. Isn't that what is more important? And how can you of all people not understand?"

Leena's nostrils flared as she took a deep breath. "Yes, I am the one who understands this perfectly. After I married Polly's father, do you know how much I had to struggle to be accepted, by not only the family but society in general? I had my in-laws breathing down my neck just waiting for me to make a mistake. I had to walk on eggshells for years. I was miserable! This badly affected my marriage also. An inter-community, inter-faith marriage is not a joke. I don't want Polly to suffer as his father or I did."

"Times have changed now, Leena", Pamela soothed, "you had no choice but to live with your in-laws. Now you will be the in-law, you can let Polly and his wife live in a separate house."

Leena's eyes widened and her necked jerked on impulse, "What? He is my only son, my only child! How can you suggest separating him from me?"

"My Neville lives away from me," Pamela offered, "It's not that bad."

Leena snorted in disdain. "Oh please, Pamela! Is that why you crib so bitterly about your daughter-in-law to me? You never have anything good to say about her, even though I think that she is quite a sensible and nice girl."

Pamela scoffed, "That's because you don't know her. You don't know how scheming she is and what she did to separate my Neville from me," she replied in an emotionally charged voice.

"That's because Neville was such a mama's boy! She probably had no other choice!" Leena shot back.

Pamela almost jumped out of her chair in anger. She glared at Leena, who glared back at her in defiance. She knew very well that she had hit upon Pamela's raw nerve. But she thought that it was well deserved.

"I thought that I would help you get Polly settled," Pamela said flatly, "but forget it!" She strode out of Leena's house in anger without as much as a second glance.

In the days to follow, a cold war ensued between Pamela and Leena. The two women had otherwise spoken to each other every day, but now they turned their faces away from one another even in church. Pamela grew morose and grumpy at home and Percy was forced to tread cautiously around her. He suggested going out for dinner to 'O Pescador' to lighten the mood. Pamela went along but the sight of Polly and Glory dampened her mood, and she lost her appetite. After that, things at home had gotten tenser. Pamela said that she did not wish to go to 'O Pescador' again. They would simply have to find a new haunt. She had come to regret her decision to help Polly which caused this whole mess. But she was too stubborn to admit to herself that she had done anything wrong.

Two months later, it was Percy's birthday. Pamela cooked up a feast like she did every year. They would have a few close friends over for dinner. Nobody was ever formally invited. The people who were closest to them simply showed up. Leena and her husband were always among them. And what's more, Leena always brought dessert, which had never been Pamela's strong suit. Pamela was quite sure that this year Leena and her husband would not turn up. She would just serve store-bought chocolate cake and vanilla ice cream this year.

Evening came and the guests began arriving. Pamela's heart skipped a beat in anticipation every time she heard Percy's booming voice welcome somebody. But there was no sign of Leena. After a couple of hours, Pamela was done making her rounds, serving little platters of croquettes, resois and chutney sandwiches. She followed it up with dainty little cups of creamy caldo verde. She was back in the kitchen busy ladling out the food into serving platters and dishes for dinner. She had come to realize that she missed Leena, indeed had been missing her all along. Leena was always there at all their family functions and Pamela was always at all of theirs. Pamela silently berated herself for expecting Leena at all.

She had just finished garnishing a large dish of fish mayonnaise with pitted green olives and sliced tomatoes when she felt a gentle pat on her shoulder. She turned around and found Leena standing there with a large bowl of her famous seradura. She felt happiest than she had in weeks. She let out an emotional cry, as though a dam inside of her had been overcome by powerful forces, "Oh Leena!" She took the dessert bowl from her friend and then embraced her tightly.

"I am sorry", they both uttered to each other simultaneously. Then they laughed nervously. Leena quickly picked up where Pamela had left off. The two of them had dinner set out in no time.

"Pamela, you have outdone yourself again!" Leena beamed as she gazed at the feast before them – prawn pulao, chicken cafreal, sorpotel, assado, fish mayonnaise and two types of fancy salads along with a basket of neatly cut katreache pao. For dessert, there was chocolate cake and vanilla ice cream in addition to Leena's large bowl of seradura. The guests were invited to encircle the table. The birthday boy stood proudly by his wife, son, daughter-in-law, and grandson while everyone chimed in with the birthday song. After he blew out his candle, there was loud applause from the guests and Pamela seized the moment to remove herself from the limelight and join Leena. Pamela's daughter-in-law was wearing a loud outfit that made her look ridiculous. Pamela gave

Leena a nudge and a knowing look and they both shared a hearty chuckle.

When they finally found themselves alone later in the evening, the two friends shared a heartfelt conversation. Pamela apologized for meddling. Leena apologized for not appreciating Pamela's well-intended help. "I have given Polly and Glory my blessing", Leena said. "If she is the only girl who can steer him into marriage, then so be it! I spoke to him and told him as much and that I want to meet her. You know, he looked shocked and denied everything. I went out of my way to convince him that I was fine with it." Leena explained. "Now let's see what happens," she smiled with a soft sigh. Pamela looked pleased and patted Leena's arm. "It will be fine", she reassured her.

The next morning, Pamela was in high spirits. Not only was her party a huge success, but she had also made up with her friend. The doorbell rang unexpectedly. Pamela found herself face to face with Polly. His face was drawn in anxiety and his normally sparkling eyes were dull with despair. Pamela greeted him warmly. He offered her a weak smile in return. She sensed that something was amiss and quickly ushered him into her hall. She thrust a cup of steaming hot coffee into his hands and took a seat opposite his. "What's the matter, Polly? Did something happen?" she asked, her voice full of concern.

"M'am," he began shakily still referring to her as he had done back in school. "What did you tell mummy about Glory and me? She thinks that something is going on between us and has again started nagging me about marriage. M'am, I tried so hard to get away from the subject of marriage and you.." he was rambling. His hands were clasped firmly together.

Pamela has never seen him so anxious. "Polly," she interrupted firmly. "Don't you like Glory? I have seen the way you are always looking at her."

"No, no M'am! I don't like her at all. I never have and I never will. She already has a boyfriend!" he asserted.

Pamela was flustered. "Then why are you always looking at her?" she demanded angrily.

Polly furrowed his brow as if he was trying to solve a complex equation.

Pamela continued, "I have seen you stare at her across the room at the restaurant," she insisted.

When realization dawned, he said, "I don't watch her M'am. I just watch the television that is mounted just behind her station."

Pamela was dumbfounded. "You mean you don't like her?"

"No, M'am!" Polly answered almost shouting. "But now mummy is on and on about me getting married again. She just doesn't get it. It's not that I don't love anyone. I do! But he..."

He? Pamela gasped.

"Polly, stop!" she shouted. She wanted to steer clear of this conversation at once. She did not want to further entangle herself in this mess. "Please speak about this directly to your mother, not me. I am sorry for the misunderstanding with Glory", she said in an agitated voice. She was embarrassed and afraid to even look Polly in the eye.

Polly was silent for a moment. When Pamela lifted her gaze to meet his, she found him staring at her with a strange expression. It was as if he had an epiphany. Then he gave her a strange smile and said, "M'am, you can't wash your hands off this now. You have gotten me into this mess and only you can get me out. It is your responsibility. Mummy is so rigid and set in her ways, but only you could get her to see past the community barrier. Maybe, you can get her to see beyond something bigger..."

Pamela was stumped. 'Oh, why the hell did I ever get involved in this nonsense?' she could not help but think.

10

Unconditional

It was an unusual Monday morning for the employees of the BB Group. The head office was abuzz! No one was in the mood to get any work done. The air was crackling with nervous energy. Imelda Braganza was dead. But that was not all. She had committed suicide on Sunday morning and had been discovered in the afternoon by her son, Bonifacio Braganza Jr., the founder and managing director of the BB group.

The local dailies were aflame with news and speculation: 'Society Queen commits suicide: Why?' She had always been a glamorous lady all the way into her seventies. She had been given centre stage at every one of her only son's many accomplishments – the unveiling of every one of their high-end real estate projects or the inauguration of their three luxury resorts. Mother and son had always enjoyed the limelight together. While Bonifacio was hailed as a business magnate, his mother was revered for her role as the family matriarch, icon of style and beacon of charity. And now, she was dead by her own hand and her son had gone into hiding. But there were more shocking revelations to come.

By afternoon, it was discovered that Bonifacio Braganza was no longer the principal owner of the assets of the BB group. The sale had been curated by a thoughtful and meticulous hand. The employees of the BB group were rattled and scared. The media was intrigued. Had Bonifacio Braganza Jr. murdered his brilliant mother and absconded with the proceeds of the massive sale of the family legacy? After all, why would the woman who had everything take her own life? The scandal fed the ravenous cravings of the media for several days to come until Bonifacio was discovered hiding somewhere in southern India. He was arrested for the alleged murder of his mother and ceremoniously escorted back to Goa where he was rigorously questioned. He vehemently denied having anything to do with his mother's death. He claimed that he had loved her to the extent of naming her as the owner of all of his assets. And it was she who had surreptitiously sold it all and donated every penny of the proceeds to her various charities. She had left him with almost nothing – no money and no answers. He could not fathom why she would do something like this.

In their last conversation, which had been telephonic, she had only asked him to visit her alone for a Sunday lunch. He was crushed by the bitter realization that it was only so that he would be the one to discover her lifeless corpse. When he'd arrived at their ancestral mansion, where she'd lived alone, there was not a soul around. She had dismissed the household staff for the day. He was certain that she had methodically planned her death and its consequences. But why had she not left him a letter or anything that would explain her bizarre actions? All that she had beside her was her bible. He had submitted it as evidence to the police. He asserted that he was innocent, but he could not explain the reason behind his mother's shocking suicide. He said that he felt utterly betrayed by her actions. She had taken away everything from him. Many, who knew the family well, would argue that Imelda had only taken away from her son, what he had earned all thanks to her. But of course, this was lost on him now.

Imelda had been the sole heir of her late father's vast estate. He had been a mighty 'bhatkar' in every sense of the word, from the vast tracts of land he owned to the multitude of tenants he harboured and employed. Her mother, Elsa, had died giving birth to her younger brother when she had been just three years old. The infant boy had been very frail and sickly. Even though her father had tried his very best to care for his infant son, the boy died at the tender age of two. Imelda had come to be her father's entire world. How he had adored her! She had been treated like a princess and had been given the best of everything that her wealthy father could provide – the finest clothes, jewellery and education.

By the time she came of age, she was proficient in the piano, and she had completed her licieu, which was the equivalent of a junior college education during Portuguese times. Her father had wished for her to study more but her mind was not in it, and he had simply let it slide. She had the most eligible of men seek her hand in marriage, but she had turned them all away along with their wealth and their titles for a handsome young man from humble roots who had been her childhood love. And yet again, her father had accepted her decision without question and had opened his arms and his home to her new husband. The only condition that he had was that the young couple should continue to reside with him in the palatial mansion that was the Braganza homestead.

Imelda could not have been more pleased. Convincing her husband to live at her father's house had been easy enough. She loved their house and would not have had it any other way, especially given her husband's humble circumstances.

The mansion was called Solar Dos Braganzas. It stood on the bank of a rivulet and boasted an amazing view of the water on one side of the home, while on the other green fields ruffled in the wind as far as the eye could see. The wind would caress the river of green grass which would gracefully glide in its direction. Imelda fancied their mansion to be an island standing tall amid all that fluidity. Everything that surrounded the house as far as the eye could see belonged to her father, even the hillocks that stood at the horizon.

As with the bhatkars of old, he did not hold a typical job. His calling was to manage his land and the tenants who resided on it. Imelda knew him to be a scholar for he was always reading and writing. He had scores of journals lying all about the house. She would at times sneak a peek into the pages filled with his elegant hand, all in Portuguese. She would find ledgers and lists interspersed with his observations of the nature, of his thoughts on life. Imelda would marvel at his refined mind. Her father would always be the man she admired most in the world.

Imelda's husband, Jacinto, was a meek man in comparison. But she had grossly underestimated the magnitude of his pride. He had begun to fill emasculated in the Braganza household, living in the towering shadow of his father-in-law. A few months into their marriage, he begged Imelda to leave with him. He had dreams he wanted to pursue in the city and of course, he wanted to get as far as possible from his wife's father. Imelda refused.

Jacinto packed up and left in the middle of the night while his wife and the rest of the household were asleep. He had left behind a letter containing an ultimatum. Imelda had been furious and ashamed of the coward that he had turned out to be. But it was far too late for regret as she was already carrying his child. She swore that she would raise the child on her own just as her father had done. Then she'd had a son and Bonifacio had been ecstatic. He wrote to his estranged son-in-law and urged him to return for the sake of the child. But he received no response. A livid Imelda had given her son her father's name and surname in honour of the only reliable man in her life. And thus Bonifacio Braganza Jr. came to be.

Leonora D'Cruz was a young journalist who had been tasked with covering the sensational death of

Imelda Braganza. She had been captivated by the story and had found it impossible to let go of it even after it had run its course. She was not entirely convinced that it had been a suicide. Several weeks after the incident, she sat at her desk mulling over the content on her laptop screen as she scrolled through several articles about the mysterious suicide. Imelda's estrangement from her husband and their early separation were all public information. It had been a little over a week since Bonifacio Jr. had been discovered in hiding and disclosed that his mother had essentially given away the family fortune. The case was rapidly growing cold. The police had already declared her death to be a suicide. But Leonora was determined to do an investigative piece on the incident. It had the potential to make a very interesting story. Her editor was not keen on the idea. After all, the paper was just a small Goan daily and there were other more current stories to cover. However, Leonora had managed to persuade him to let her pursue the story on her own time. She was determined to see it through.

As part of her meticulous plan for the investigation, she first revisited her source at the police station that had handled the investigation. He had confirmed that there was no suicide note found alongside the body, just a well-worn leather-bound bible that was believed to be Imelda's. However, he had initially refused to let her have a look at the evidence. But now that the case had been closed as a suicide and the story had gone cold in the press, Leonora had been able to convince him to let her examine the bible.

When she entered the dusty evidence room, she could barely contain her excitement. The Bible was contained in a plastic Ziploc bag. She donned a pair of latex gloves and gently removed the old book from the bag. It was a thick book bound in black leather and Leonora resisted the urge to take a long sniff from its pages for she loved the smell of old books, especially ones which were cherished and preserved. She opened the pages with reverence and found Imelda's name written on one of the front pages in a bold cursive hand that had faded a little. This confirmed the ownership of the holy book.

Leonora carefully looked through the pages of the bible and found three holy pictures which had been given out as souvenirs at three distinct funerals. These were probably being used as bookmarks. But the most interesting find was an old black-and-white photograph of a beautiful young girl, standing alongside a distinguished elderly gentleman. The girl was a young Imelda and the man beside her was her late father, Bonifacio Sr. A date was inscribed behind the photograph in faded blue ink.

Leonora closely looked through every single page hoping to find clues – passages that may have been underlined or notes that may have been scribbled in the margins. But there was absolutely nothing to be found. After she was completely satisfied with this fact, Leonora replaced the contents of the bible and placed it back in the plastic bag. She returned the evidence bag to its custodian. She knew everything about the current investigation which amounted to nothing new. The autopsy revealed that Imelda had consumed an overdose of a strong sedative with port wine. There were no signs of any kind of struggle, no signs of a break-in or an intruder.

Leonora's next step was to visit the scene of the crime – the ancestral mansion where Imelda had taken her life. The lady had not spared even the ancestral mansion. It had been sold to a group that specialized in restoring old palaces, mansions and such and running them as boutique hotels. It seemed to Leonora that Imelda had taken special efforts to leave her childhood home with caring custodians. Had she not trusted her son to do the same? It was as though she had been determined to leave him with nothing. Why? Leonora felt that the answer to this question was the key to the mystery behind Imelda's death. She had contacted the Braganza's estate lawyer, but their lips were irrevocably sealed. She knew not to expect any answers from them.

When Leonora arrived at what was now the former Braganza family mansion, she found that it had been transformed. The new owners certainly hadn't wasted any time. Leonora could hear the sounds of steady hammering, drilling, and polishing in the background. The mansion had been emptied of its contents; the mere shell of it was being renovated. Leonora looked around and decided that finding anything of use in the mansion itself was a lost cause.

She stepped out of the large compound and found three little houses standing close to each other. Leonora had a hunch that perhaps the neighbours would know a little more about the Braganza story. She was proved correct. One of the residents was an octogenarian by the name of Lucia. She had been a long-time employee of the Braganza household before retiring when she was almost seventy. She had been employed by the Braganzas ever since Bonifacio Jr. had been a baby and had helped Imelda raise him. Imelda was close to her and continued to visit her even after she had retired from service.

Lucia was a lonely old woman who was deeply saddened by the loss of Imelda whom she considered to be more a friend than an employer. Leonora was gentle with her and encouraged her to speak freely. Lucia was more than happy to share her stories. She had nothing but high praise for her former mistress – her beauty, her strength, and her generosity. But with Bonifacio Jr. or 'Bonnie' as he was called, her affection did not run as deep. She recalled that he had been an unruly child whose mischief was borderline sadism – from teasing helpless animals to tripping hapless servants.

Lucia recounted several incidents to cite examples of Bonnie's misdeeds. "He always pulled out the latches of all the doors and left them sticking out like that. There were so many times I scrapped myself against those things. Our bhatkar began calling him Houdini. I didn't know who that was, but then Imelda bai explained that Houdini was a famous magician who would escape from locked boxes and things. Bonnie baba did not like being teased and bitterly complained to Imelda bai until she asked our bhatkar to stop it." Lucia recalled.

Leonora encouraged Lucia to tell more of her stories. She spoke about the time that Bonnie turned twenty-one. Imelda gifted him a car. "Bai had planned the gift many many months ahead of time. She was more excited to give Bonnie baba the car than he was to receive it," she smiled fondly at the thought. "But Bonnie baba crashed the car within a week. Luckily no one was hurt. He smashed the car against a tree because he was drunk. That new car was completely ruined. But bai was more relieved that Bonnie was safe. So much money she spent on that car! Tsk tsk", Lucia shook her head.

She went on to tell Leonora that the accident had been the final straw for Bonifacio Sr. He had a heated argument with Imelda. He even threatened to cut off Bonnie as well as Imelda from his will. He blamed her for spoiling him rotten. Father and daughter were not on speaking terms in the days that followed. Before they could make up, he had been found dead. There had been a small police investigation but, in the end, it had been concluded that Bonifacio Sr., who was well into his eighties, had died of old age and peacefully in his sleep. After that, Imelda inherited everything. Bonnie had effectively been handed the keys to the kingdom. With the unflinching support of his mother, he had gone on to build his business empire on his grandfather's wealth. "No mother could be as proud of her son, as my bai", Lucia exclaimed. She also admitted that Imelda had been very shaken by her father's death. She was not only deeply saddened by it but disturbed somehow. Lucia felt that Imelda had never been the same since Bonifacio Sr.'s death.

Leonora asked Lucia when she had last seen Imelda. "Bai came to see me a few days before she died. She seemed to be very upset. When I asked, she told me that she had found something very disturbing. She held some papers in her hand. She was agitated, looking at those papers again and again. But she wouldn't say anything else. When she left, she forgot the papers on my table. I called out after her to take the papers with her. But she just told me to burn them." Lucia exclaimed.

Leonora felt that she was very close to a breakthrough. With bated breath, she asked Lucia what she had done with the papers.

"I kept them. I thought that they may be important and bai would want them back," Lucia replied.

Leonora could not believe her ears, "Can you show them to me?"

Lucia withdrew a folder bunch of papers from under the floral plastic tablecloth that adorned the small table that was within her reach.

"Can you please do me a favour?" she asked Leonora. "I am old and may die soon. Can you please take these papers and give them to Bonnie baba? Tell him that bai left them with me."

Leonora asked Lucia if she could look at the papers herself. Lucia simply shrugged. Leonora thanked the old lady and left. She almost ran to her car and opened the papers. They were old and delicate. They were yellowing certificates, all in Portuguese and she could make no sense of them. She would have to get them reviewed back at the office. What she discovered was nothing short of a revelation!

That night, back at home, Leonora went through her notes and tried to put together all that she had found. The old papers left behind by Imelda proved that Imelda was not the biological daughter of Bonifacio Sr. She had been adopted by him at the age of one when her widowed mother had remarried Bonifacio Sr. Judging from what Lucia had told her, it would seem that Imelda had not known about this before. It must have certainly been a shock to find out that the man she had considered to be her father, was not. But this news was not nearly distressing enough to have led her to take her own life. Was it? Why?

Leonora stayed up all night sifting through the possibilities. She had done all her homework on Imelda. She knew about her privileged upbringing, wherein she had been cocooned by the love of a devoted father. Imelda had hit a rough patch with the dissolution of her marriage, but that had been countered by the birth of her son whom she had adored above all else. Her father's death had been a hard blow, but again she'd clung on to her son who had carried her along on his road to success. She did not appear to have any history of depression. Towards the end, she discovered that she had been adopted by a father who had treated her no differently than his own flesh and blood. The only thing that her father had faulted her with was being an overindulgent mother. Leonora wondered whether

Imelda had something to do with her father's death. That would explain her guilt. But why did she financially ruin her son? Did they have a falling out over money? That didn't add up since everything was in her name anyway. It was clear that Bonifacio Jr. had trusted his mother completely.

Leonora finally succumbed to sleep in the wee hours of the morning. Her slumber calmed her mind. She awoke a couple of hours later to the sound of her phone alarm with a mild headache and a small hunch. Later in the day, she visited the police station in the village where Bonifacio Sr. had been born and had died. She asked for the officer who had dealt with the investigation into the old man's death twenty years ago. By an amazing stroke of luck, he was still around. He had only been recently transferred back to the same police station and was due to retire soon. Leonora told him about the story she was working on and her hunch. He was intrigued and agreed to help her out of sheer curiosity. He found the thin file on Bonifacio Sr's death. It consisted of a few statements from Imelda and a few servants. It was a maid who had found him dead in his bed. He had suffered from a minor heart attack a few days before his death and for that reason, it was suspected that he had suffered a heart attack and died peacefully in his sleep. There was no autopsy done. The case was closed.

There were two sepia-tinted black and white photographs enclosed in the file. One was a picture of the inside of Bonifacio Sr's bedroom in which he had died. It showcased an ornate four-postered bed with a white canopy. It was unmade with its pillows and covers in disarray. The other was a picture taken from outside the room, at its entrance. It showed the big open double door of the bedroom, with its latch left jutting out. Leonora found the photo very odd and asked the police officer about it. "Oh that?" the police officer said, "I took the photograph because it was just so strange to see that heavy latch sticking out like that when the door had never been closed or locked. Mr. Braganza, it seems, never closed his bedroom door, not even at night. Plus, that heavy latch was on the outside of the door. "

Leonora decided to do one last thing before concluding her story. She had to meet the last remaining actor in the play. It was not easy getting an appointment with Bonifacio Jr. He looked like the shell of the man he once was. But there was still an air of defiance about him. She explained to him that she had been working on a story about his mother's death. She placed the thin sheath of papers that she had obtained from Lucia on his table. She knew that he was fluent in Portuguese.

"These are for you", she said. He looked at her lamely and began looking through them. Then she added, "Your mother discovered her true parentage quite recently. It appears that she was adopted by Bonifacio Sr. And of course, she knew what you had done to the man who had raised her as his child and who had loved her unconditionally. The burden must have finally become too much to bear."

Leonora watched as for the briefest moment, an expression of pure horror appeared like a shadow across Bonifacio's face and disappeared just as quickly. Blandly he said to her, "I really don't know what you are talking about."

11

Athi Sundar

Present Day

Vishnu carefully placed the bamboo ladder against the hood of his orange truck. Then he climbed up, wet rag in hand and began wiping the windshield in a circular motion. He gently rubbed the name 'Laxmi' painted on the upper right-hand corner to remove the fine filament of dust that had gathered there. The name had not only been a tribute to the goddess of wealth but also to his late wife who he had adored. Since the time his wife had crossed the threshold of his home, she had brought the family good fortune. She had borne him a son, although he was to be their only child. What a child he had been! And now it seemed that after her death two years ago, the blessings from the goddess of wealth had left along with her. His beloved son had left the house much before her passing and now Vishnu was left alone.

It had been more than a year since mining operations in the area had been brought to a halt by a series of court orders which were passed to curb illegal mining activities in the state of Goa. Yet Vishnu cared for his truck and tended to her for she was a poignant reminder of everything that had once been good in his life.

HiStory

As was the custom in the old days, he was married very young. His wife had been even younger. His parents had both been hard-working farmers. They had never received an education, but they had given their all to ensure that Vishnu and his older brother Vijay had gone to school. Both the boys had successfully matriculated and to them, this must have seemed like a huge feat and the fruition of all their efforts.

Vijay had obediently taken to the fields as was expected of him. But Vishnu had always been restless. He knew of friends and relatives who had made a lot of money working in the Gulf. The jobs there certainly paid much more than what he would ever make out of farming. He thought that his parents and his brother were foolish to not be able to see beyond farming – all that back-breaking labour in the paddy fields for a pittance! And so, a little more than a year after his marriage, after Laxmi had given him a son, he managed to make his way to the Gulf. He ended up doing manual labour on various construction sites. He dutifully sent home some money every month, but even so, managed to save up a decent nest egg.

His living quarters were cramped as he shared it with three other Indian men, all in situations similar to his. But he adapted. He had a plan and a goal of his own. He could afford to travel home once every two years or so. He would go back loaded with gifts for everyone. The sheer delight on their faces as they reverently handled the foreign goods, he had brought for them, made it all worthwhile. In their eyes, he was a big man, a city man.

Vishnu especially revelled in the adoration of his wife, Laxmi, and son Sundar. How aptly named his son had been. Sundar means beautiful. The child was indeed gorgeous. Fair and chubby with thick black curls. He was the envy of every mother in their village. Laxmi never took him out of the house, without putting a black tika on his forehead or cheek to ward off the evil eye. So smitten was Laxmi with her baby son, that she would gaze at him adoringly and sigh out loud, "Sundar, athi sundar." It was a Hindi phrase which translates into 'Beautiful, very beautiful.'

Vishnu spent close to a decade toiling away in the gulf. Then his parents died in quick succession, and he knew that it was time to come home. Vishnu's parents had left their two sons a few acres of farmland and their modest ancestral house. The two brothers divided the land equally amongst themselves. Vijay offered to farm Vishnu's share of the land since Vishnu clearly had no intention of doing so himself. But Vishnu declined out of pride. He had saved up a little nest egg which he felt certain was enough to provide for his family, until such time that Sundar was old enough to take over the reins. So confident was he that he decided to give up the family house and build one of his own.

The family lived comfortably off Vishnu's savings for a few years. But by the time Sundar was in his early teens, Vishnu came to realize that his nest egg was depleting faster than he had anticipated. He needed to find some gainful employment to supplement the monthly allowance from his savings. He had a great desire to see his son not only matriculate but graduate from college as well. But little did he know that Sundar had other ideas.

The beautiful child had developed into a handsome young man, tall with chiseled features and a deep resonating voice. Sundar was admired for his good looks by everyone he encountered, and he loved basking in all those appreciative glances. He fancied himself the next Bollywood superstar and secretly harboured dreams of making it big there. He had confided about his dream to only one person – his biggest fan and enabler, his mother.

Laxmi catered to her only son's every whim and fancy. She bought him everything he ever wanted which included good clothes and accessories. She also gave him a very generous pocket allowance. She had even been planning on buying him a motorcycle on his eighteenth birthday. All she needed to do was to convince Vishnu to shell out the cash, which was rather easy for her. She was blissfully unaware of the state of their dwindling finances.

For as long as he could remember, there were mining activities had taken place in his village. But the operations were relatively small. Vishnu decided to take a risk and buy himself a truck. He would thus become self-employed and get himself engaged in the transportation of iron ore from the mines to the barges. Things were relatively slow at first, but in the early part of the new millennium, the demand for iron ore from

China surged. Now it seemed that everyone wanted to get their fingers into the mining pie – from ambitious politicians to shady operators. Many of the new mining operations were illegal. But of course, money could make the impossible, possible.

Vishnu's investment paid off. He had more work than he could handle. Pretty soon, it seemed like every family in his village purchased a truck and went into business. As Vishnu would like to say, "It does not matter if they don't have a proper roof over their heads, but they have a truck!" Traditional occupations such as farming were quickly abandoned for mining activities which paid far better. Fields thus went fallow. Age-old water bodies dried up because subterranean water tables were altered due to mining. Mining companies began supplying locals with water tankers. Everything from trees to houses was covered in red dust. But people did not mind any of it. Red had come to be the new colour of money.

'Businessmen' began purchasing large tracts of land from locals at astronomical prices the likes of which the locals had never seen before. Even Vishnu's brother, who had been a devoted farmer, had been offered a sum so large that he was left with no option but to sell his land. When Vishnu heard about the sale, he could not believe what his brother had done. 'Lucky fool! He has made enough to have the next two generations in his family live in comfort.' Vishnu thought to himself. He prayed that his land would fetch a similar offer.

A few days after Vijay's big sale, Vishnu was sitting outside his house staring at the ripening evening sky while sipping a cup of hot tea. Laxmi was inside the house busy preparing dinner. He was surprised to see the silhouette of his brother approaching the house. The straight and steady gait was unmistakable. When Vijay reached the house, he sat down next to his younger brother without an invitation. Vishnu could sense Vijay's anxiety. He simply waited in silence for his brother to speak up.

"Vishnu, hanv atam kitem korum?" he cried out in a dejected tone.

(*"Vishnu, what should I do now?*)

"Hanvem aiee babak vachan dilolo to todun udoilo!"

(*I have broken the promise that I made to mother and father!*)

Vishnu knew very well that Vijay was referring to the sale of his land. Vishnu's curiosity got the better of him. Even though he did not want to upset his brother anymore, he asked him why he had sold the land in the first place. Vijay revealed that the money was just too much of a temptation for his wife and grown sons. He was against the sale. But they eventually wore him down. Vishnu sighed. It was a common tale around these parts. The two brothers continued to sit together in solemn silence after Vijay's confession. Laxmi appeared and brought Vijay a glass of water and a cup of hot tea. Vishnu caught his wife's eye and smiled at her. At that moment, he felt grateful for her kindness.

Vishnu still hoped that he would receive a handsome offer for his fields as well. He did receive a couple of offers but he felt that he could do much better if he held out for just a little longer. Besides, his financial situation was stable. He was earning quite well with his truck. If he managed to squeeze in at least two trips a day, he would earn at least a thousand rupees per day, plus he received handsome commissions from time to time.

As production of the ore increased drastically to meet the demand from the east, the need for transport grew as well. The locally available supply of truck drivers was augmented by migrants from other states. Vishnu greatly disapproved of these fellows. Most of them were not properly trained drivers. They did not even possess driver's licenses. They were paid based on the number of trips they made. They were either ignorant about basic driving rules or chose to blatantly disregard these in their race to complete as many trips as possible in a day. In their recklessness, they caused numerous accidents. It had all come to be part of the racket to make a quick buck.

When he came of age, Sundar announced that he was leaving home for Mumbai. He was going to try his luck in the film industry. Laxmi was heartbroken but supported her son's decision, nonetheless. Vishnu thought that it was utter foolishness and strongly objected to the move. But in the end, he was helpless and had to watch his son walk out of their home. Neither Vishnu nor Laxmi could bring themselves to face the fact that their only son, their pride and joy, had been a disappointment. He had failed his tenth standard exams and it had taken him two more attempts to finally clear it. He would have just given up on it, had it not been for his father.

Vishnu and Laxmi had been greatly relieved when he finally cleared his exams. But Sundar had made it very clear to them, that he had no intention of pursuing further studies. Vishnu's hopes had been dashed. But nothing would change Sundar's mind – not the long arguments with his father nor the gentle pleas of his mother. He had spent the last few years of his life whiling away his time and living off his father. Vishnu had offered to buy him a truck so that Sundar could join his father in the family business. But Sundar shunned the offer. He thought that being a truck driver was beneath him. He was certain that he was destined for greater things.

With Sundar gone, Laxmi lost her spark. She tried her best to put on a brave face for Vishnu. But he could see beyond her façade. He missed Sundar immensely himself. But he had known that at some point in time Sundar would leave the nest. He would have to face the world that he was so desperate to make his own. 'It is all in God's hands, whether he is greeted by success or failure.' Vishnu thought. He wished that Sundar could have been content to just stay at home and work with his father like countless other sons. Then he chastised himself for the double standard. He remembered how he wanted nothing to do with his own father's profession, how he had looked down on being a farmer. 'Like father, like son,' he thought bitterly. Life had indeed come full circle.

Vishnu and Laxmi tried hard to keep in touch with Sundar. But he did not make it easy for them. He seldom replied to their letters nor returned their calls. In the end, they decided to just be patient and wait for him to come back to them. Almost a year after Sundar left, Laxmi's health took a turn for the worse. She passed away whilst calling for him. Vishnu was distraught. He has lost his soul mate. Sundar finally came home to attend his mother's funeral. Vishnu could not contain his anger. "Where were you?" he demanded of his son. "She waited and waited for you and finally died. What kind of son are you?" Sundar did not utter a word in response.

After the twelfth-day mourning ritual had been completed, Vishnu had finally gathered himself. He spoke to his son again, gently this time.

He pleaded with his son. "Mhojea vangdda rav Sundar. Tukam hanga kitem kami asa?" (*Stay with me Sundar. What is it that you lack here?*)

But Sundar was adamant about leaving. He did not get into an argument with his father but wordlessly left home. Vishnu was left alone. Laxmi's medical expenses had taken a huge toll on his finances, plus he was still supporting Sundar financially. He would religiously send him a small amount every month to help him with living expenses. He had begun to do so at Laxmi's urging, even though Sundar had never asked for it. Now he couldn't bring himself to stop. It seemed like the money was the only link that he had to his son. Thank goodness for the truck. It was the only reliable thing in his life at this point. But a few months later, another tragedy struck when mining operations were brought to a halt by a court order. His mission to obtain financial stability for both Sundar and him was brutally upended.

Veteran mining companies were forced to withdraw operations. Fly-by-night operators simply cut their losses, closed shop, and scampered away. Migrant labour that had flocked to mining haven, left for greener pastures. The people who were truly left behind holding the proverbial baby were the locals. The trucking business had completely dried up and the useless vehicles were left parked all about the village.

With no work in sight, there was endless pain, anger, and time – time for pointless and heated discussions. Local leaders provided the outlets for protests and marches. The government made promises about resuming mining in a few months, which turned into more months and months. Vishnu who had initially been a vociferous advocate to resume mining operations had lost all hope and faith. He confined himself to his empty house, doing nothing but sleeping all day.

One of Vjay's daughters-in-law, Tulsi, brought him two square meals a day. He felt obliged to eat and stay alive. But it was a painful reminder of the fact that he was the recipient of his brother's charity. He still resented his brother for being one of the few lucky ones who had made his money before the whole thing had gone bust.

Present Day

One evening there was a knock on the door. Vishnu thought it was probably his nephew's wife bringing him his dinner. But when he opened the door, he found Vijay there instead. He had brought along the tiffin boxes neatly wrapped in muslin. Vishnu had last seen his brother at Laxmi's funeral.

"Tulsi could not come today, so I thought that I should bring you the food myself," Vijay said hesitantly. Vishnu wordlessly followed Vijay into the house and remained silent until Vijay left a few moments later.

From that day on, it was Vijay who visited Vishnu twice a day with packed food. Gradually the ice between the two brothers began to thaw. Vishnu was secretly relieved that it had been his brother who had made the first move. He had been very lonely since Laxmi's death. He now looked forward to Vijay's visits and although not much was said, they both spent their time together in companionable silence.

They began to take walks together in the village to ward off the awkwardness. They walked through the place which was their home and for the first time Vishnu registered what he saw: how their once green village had changed, how what was once forest and farmland had been reduced to bowls of red dust. The enormous pits created by mining activities were now filled with water and had become ominous lakes. The springs of his childhood had run dry. He was forced to acknowledge that things had spiralled out of control in the past few years. He realized that he had been too indifferent to assimilate the price of greed.

That year, the monsoon arrived on time. During their long walks together, the brothers could not help but appreciate how in the absence of mining activities, nature had already begun the healing process. The rain had washed away the layers of red dust that had once covered all the trees and shrubbery. Even amidst dozens of abandoned trucks, the vegetation had begun to cover everything in its path. The fields that were left to him by his father looked green with overgrown weeds. Vishnu regarded his land closely and was struck by a thought. Here was his way out of the financial hole. He could cultivate the land which had originally been paddy fields. The soil was well-rested and replenished. It was worth a shot; at least he wouldn't have to count on his big brother's charity forever. He could get back his dignity as a man. He mentioned it to Vijay there and then. The announcement took Vijay by surprise. He had never thought that he would get to see his younger brother ever take to the soil. It delighted him. He assured Vishnu that he would help him in every way possible. He was anyway tired of sitting around his house, idle. It was wonderful to have a sense of purpose again.

The two of them made a plan together. A strange exuberance had set in between the brothers. It made them feel like the boys they had once been. It had just taken half a century to bring the two of them together on a common mission, not since when they stole raw mangoes and hog plums together as children. Vijay helped Vishnu hire a small tractor to till the land. They also hired a few local hands to help out. Vishnu discovered that he had not forgotten how to do fieldwork. All those years of working side by side his parents had left a lasting impression.

A few weeks later, the paddy crop stood tall and proud waving in the post-monsoon heat. Vishnu could just imagine the look on his parents' faces had they been around to see the day when he could harvest his first crop. His aiee-baba would have finally been truly proud of him. As he admired the fruits of his labour, he took a deep breath of the air sweetened by his ripening crop. 'Athi Sundar', he thought to himself.

12

Rooster on the Roof

I could not help but smile as the old Portuguese-era house drew nearer. The ancient mango tree that shielded the house from view withdrew into the background as I marched my way towards it. The house was a one-storied structure with sturdy wooden verandahs that stretched from end to end on both floors. On the ground floor, the two main pillars that propped the upper verandah were draped with a pretty climber plant that bore tiny orange trumpet-shaped flowers. The large bulky front door of the house was wide open as always. It would only be closed at night once all of the house's inhabitants were safely back in.

It was the summer of 1998 and I had just turned eighteen. This was the house that my aunt, my godmother, had been married into, in the quaint village of Siolim. Her name was Rosaline, but I had always called her Rosie. I was to spend the next two weeks in her house with her husband's family as I had done every summer for the past five years. It was an experience that I had always cherished. This particular vacation was especially poignant. I had hoped that it would diminish all my worries about what the future held, while I waited for the results of my Standard twelfth board examination.

I crossed the threshold proffered by the compound gate into the long narrow yard that eventually opened into a wide compound that encircled the whole house. The mud path that led to the house was flanked on both sides by a pretty garden with rows of flowering plants. Through the open front door, I could see all the way back to the main dining hall on the ground floor of the house and catch a sliver of the old staircase that led to the upper floor.

"Henri!" my aunt called out, the moment she laid her eyes on me. Henri was short for Henrietta, and it was what everyone called me. I preferred it to the old-fashioned English name that my parents had bestowed upon me. Rosie galloped towards me and hugged me with one arm whilst taking my travel bag with the other. She beckoned me to follow her to the room I knew so well because I'd spent the last five summers in it.

I crossed the antique cupboard in the hallway with its large mirror and took a peek at myself. Everyone commented that I had grown taller. My short curly hair had become even more unruly from the sixty-minute bus ride. I still bore the tan that I had acquired from playing basketball, even though I had been on vacation for more than a month. I looked at my chubby face in the mirror and smiled into my own eyes. I loved my eyes. They were a shade of golden brown and were my best feature. I was told that the shade was called hazel. I had been overcome by my vanity for a moment but shrugged it off quickly to go unpack and get on with the rest of my day.

But first things first, I had to pay my respects to the matriarch of the family – my aunt's mother-in-law, whom I had taken to calling Avozinha. She was tall and wore a boyish crop of silver hair. She stood in the kitchen with her usual ramrod-straight posture, whilst supervising the cooking. Her helpers scurried around her. For a woman in her seventies, she was still as sharp as a tack and just as warm. She hugged me as soon as I had greeted her and instructed my aunt to give me a bowl of vegetable soup that had been simmering on the fire.

Suddenly, there was a loud screech. It was the sound of an electric guitar. Poor Avozinha dropped the spoon she had been holding in fright.

"Malcriado!" she murmured through gritted teeth.

The sound had been only momentary, and she soon regained her composure. Rosie led me out of the kitchen quickly. "What was that?" I asked her. "I'll tell you all about it later," she whispered.

I gradually met all the members of the large family through the course of the day – my uncle, his two bachelor brothers and his youngest sister. Meals were always consumed together at the large dining table that could seat ten. I didn't do much else that day, except unpack and take a long nap in the afternoon. I was going to enjoy being lazy during these holidays.

The next morning everyone except Rosie and Avozinha strode off to work. My aunt was a school teacher and that was one of the reasons that I could spend my holidays with her. After breakfast, she left me to my own devices and went about her routine. I rushed off to the first floor which was the part of the house that I preferred. Most of it was a large living room with comfortable old sofas and a row of three French windows on one side. It opened out into the verandah at the front of the house through another pair of French windows. Adjoining it was a small bedroom which was used by one of my uncle's brothers. He was an avid collector of comics and let me borrow his stash during my time there. This was another thing that I loved about this place – I was hardly ever bored, not after having access to a year's supply of comics.

I quickly grabbed a couple of comics and made my way to the most interesting part of the house. There was a special window at the back of the living room. One could climb out of it and land straight on the tiled roof that covered the back portion of the house. The top floor of the house only covered the front portion of the house. Atop its pyramidal tiled roof stood an ancient earthen rooster, a sentinel at its post for what must have easily been over a century. The roof was a wonderful place to sit and read. It overlooked a sea of green coconut tree fronds on one side, and on the other offered a clear view of the side of the neighbouring house.

Ah! The house next door! It was even grander than Avozinha's house. It did not have a top floor, but its ceiling was so high that it nearly matched Avozinha's house in height. The front of the house bore majestic, tall French windows painted white. The house was just a few meters apart from Avozinhas. It was so close that if I stood at the French windows at the side of the hall upstairs, I could see straight down into their hall.

From what I could see, their furniture was ornate, antique, and lovingly maintained. Their garden upfront was beautifully kept with two large fan-like palms covering the façade. It made their house seem like a lady covering her beautiful face from view with fans. I knew a little about the neighbours who lived in that gorgeous house. They were an elegant old couple who could afford to keep a small army of helpers to assist in its meticulous maintenance. Avozinha had told me that they had a son who had settled abroad with his family.

I gazed at the neighbouring house for a little while before settling into my corner of the roof. It was hot yet breezy and I thought that I had been wise to don a pair of shorts and a loose cotton T-shirt. I placed the cushion that I had brought with me on a section of the tiles that was sloping down and made myself comfortable. I had a good view of a short airy corridor at the side of the house. It had large windows that opened outward, and it probably flanked a small rozangno.

I opened my first comic and was soon engrossed. I was done with it in no time at all. When I looked up, I was startled to see a figure moving slowly across the neighbour's corridor. I had been staring at the pages of the comic which were illuminated by the sunlight for far too long. I was seeing spots before my eyes and could discern just the shadow of a figure standing there and possibly looking up at me. I immediately jumped up and scampered away back into the hall through the back window. 'Wow, that was strange!" I told myself. It was getting quite hot on the roof anyway and I would be better off reading in the living room. I settled into a comfortable sofa with my comics.

'Yaaa…eeeee!' I almost jumped. There it was again – the strangled cry of an electric guitar. The sounds were coming from somewhere in the house next door. It was quite loud indeed. No wonder Avozinha had been upset. However, after a few initial electric shrieks, there was music being played and it sounded pretty good. I relaxed and resumed reading. I remembered that Rosie was supposed to fill me in on the mysterious music yesterday, but we had never gotten around to it. I would surely ask her about it today. The chance to do so presented itself much sooner than expected. I heard raised voices coming from outside. I couldn't hear what was being said because of the ongoing music. But it was enough to know that it was an angry exchange. It stopped a moment later and soon after I heard a woman's voice calling angrily, "Noah! Noah! Turn that sound down!"

The volume of the music did dip a notch, but I doubted that it was enough to satisfy the aggrieved parties. I hurried downstairs. Rosie was sitting at the dining table, sifting through grains of uncooked rice. She saw me and beckoned me to sit beside her. I noticed that Avozinha had shut her room door. It was very unlike her to do so in the middle of the day. "What happened?" I whispered to Rosie as I pulled out a chair.

"Mummy is very upset and has locked herself in her room to rest", she answered softly. She went on to tell me that the angry exchange that I had just heard had indeed been Avozinha scolding the lady next door about the noise. They had been good friends and neighbours for decades, but things had gotten tense in the last month since their grandson had moved in and started practicing the electric guitar. And oh yes! He also played the drums on occasion. The usually serene environment had been disrupted and poor Avozinha's nerves had been frayed. She had kept it in for as long as she could. But today she had just exploded in rage. I felt so bad for Avozinha. Rosie decided to go over to the neighbour's house and mend fences. She would also request a drastic reduction in the music volume. Things were a little tense in the house for the rest of the day but eased up in the evening when, one by one, Avozinha's children began returning home. The night was quiet and uneventful. At least the maverick musician had the decency to not play at night, I thought to myself.

The next morning after breakfast, I went back upstairs and did not think twice about heading out onto the roof with my comics. It was early in the day and the morning sunlight was gentle. I settled into my spot and began to read.

"Hi there!" a man's voice called.

I instinctively looked up and then down at the neighbours' corridor. A lanky young man with beautiful long straight silken hair was smiling up at me. I thought about my wretched curls as I enviously watched him run his slender fingers through his hair and watched it glide back into place.

"I am Noah. What's your name?" he called out again.

I was staring at him with my mouth ajar and must have looked ridiculous like that. I pulled myself together momentarily.

"Henrietta" I replied, "Or just Henri."

So, this was the musical menace. I sighed. He was gorgeous. My heart sank at the thought that I was certainly not, and he was far out of my league.

"What are you reading?" he asked.

"Comics" I called back.

"Oh, heavy stuff," he said jokingly. It irked me.

"I heard you practice", I said.

"And what did you think of my music?" he asked with a slight smile.

"Too loud", I retorted. There! That would shut him up.

He shot back a devastating smile and his eyes drifted down to my bare legs. I was mortified. Oh, why did I have to wear shorts today?

"I'll see you around", he said pleasantly still wearing the killer smile. He waved at me and walked away.

My heart was racing. I sat down shakily and tried to calm it. Wow! I had never felt this way before. It was thrilling, yet it made me feel so self-conscious. I didn't think that I would be comfortable going out onto the roof again. I didn't think that I could face him again, even though I wanted to. I hurried back inside the house and did not venture out onto the roof for the rest of the day.

Was it my imagination or was the volume of music much more subdued? Rosie assured me that it indeed was much softer than usual. Avozinha's mood was back on the mend. The lady from next door had visited with a peace offering and Avozinha had melted. She must have been so worried about wrecking such an old friendship. The two ladies had agreed to have the two families unite for tea the next evening at the house next door. And I was invited as well. 'Woah! I would meet that handsome devil in person, I thought, and my heart started racing again. I was full of nervous energy afterwards and began to pace the house relentlessly. Rosie noticed and suggested that I go for a nice long walk outdoors.

The next day dawned, and I felt much calmer in the morning. But no, I would not step out onto that roof again. The anticipation began to build up gradually and by the time it was evening, I was nervous. I wore my favourite blue jeans and a very conservative-looking top. I tried to tame my curls but in vain. I just tied them into a loose ponytail as I usually did. I donned my sneakers and set out to the house next door along with Avozinha and Rosie. The rest of the family was still at work.

We entered their house through the front door. It was just as fabulous as I had been expecting. The main sala was painted in a cool refreshing shade of pale green and the room was flooded with the light coming in through its tall windows. Avozinha introduced me to Mr. and Mrs. Monteiro as Rosie's niece. That was when the devil appeared. I swallowed involuntarily and hoped that he hadn't seen that. Ha! It had been good sense to wear a blouse with such a high collar after all. Mrs. Monteiro introduced her grandson Noah to us, like a teacher introducing her naughtiest student to the headmistress. But Avozinha was very warm towards him and that put Mrs. Monteiro at ease.

Noah was smiling at everyone. But it was a demure respectable smile, not that devilish dashing smile that he had thrown me the other day. Our eyes met for a moment, but I quickly looked away. He took a seat directly across from me and my heart began racing wildly. I kept my eyes averted, fixed firmly to the floor, and occasionally let them wander to the walls. Then, Mrs. Monteiro suggested that Noah should show me the house. He jumped up and stood by me, gesturing the way ahead. I looked at him then, smiling nervously like an idiot and followed him out. He obediently gave me a grand tour of the magnificent house, whilst softly talking about every room. My body could not take the tension anymore and I simply let it go. I began to focus on my breathing and relaxed a little. He had saved his music room for last, and this was where he was the most animated.

"Do you play an instrument?" he gently asked.

"No, I have never had the ear for it", I answered. "Do you intend to pursue music as a career or is it just a hobby?"

"Career! My parents are angry as hell. But I convinced them to let me give it a try. What about you?" he asked.

I told him that I was waiting for my board results which would probably determine what I would pursue. "I guess I will just go with the flow," I said. "I don't have anything that about I am really passionate about like you do."

"Ah! Except for comics", he said and flashed that devilish smile that he had kept hidden until now.

I smiled back lamely, and we continued to talk. I grew at ease and didn't realize just how much time I had spent with him until Rosie came looking for me.

"I'll see you on the roof tomorrow morning." He whispered as I turned to follow Rosie out. I nodded with a smile and waved him goodbye. He gave me a dazzling smile that made my heart flip. That summer, I would learn that he had a different smile for every mood. But the ones used most often were the naughty devilish smile, the contemplative smile and the dazzling happy smile that would reach his eyes.

I was so happy that night and sleep came only after several failed attempts. Over the next few days, we settled into a routine: I would go up to the roof in the morning and he would be waiting for me, leaning against the corridor window with a coffee mug in his hand. There we would talk across the rooftops until the sun got too warm. In the evenings, we would go out for a walk together, exploring the beautiful neighbourhood and be back before dark. He had spent his early childhood here and had very fond memories of it. There was a rivulet that flowed not far from the house. He told me about how his grandfather used to take him crab fishing. They would use round basket-like nets and suspend a piece of bait inside before lowering it into the water. They would leave it there for an hour and then abruptly pull it out to almost always haul a good catch of crabs . His grandmother made the most delicious crab xec xec, he told me. He invited me to go crab fishing with him. I loved how he spoke so warmly of his family and so passionately about his music. He was not a devil after all. I knew that I was falling in love with him, more with every moment I spent in his company. I could not dream of telling him about my feelings for we were both on a short holiday which was bound to end in a few days. After that, we would both go our separate ways.

It was on Sunday morning, after returning from mass when Noah and I went crab fishing. He had carried along his acoustic guitar with him. He had to sling the guitar case on his back so that he could carry the crab traps plus a bucket in his hands. I offered to help but he valiantly declined. The embankment of the rivulet had been built up and was about five feet above the water level. Noah gently lowered two baited crab traps into the water and secured the ropes under two large stones. Now we had to wait, the longer the better, for a decent haul. He sat beside me on the soft grass overlooking the river. Then he wordlessly unsheathed his guitar. "My lady", he said, "This song is dedicated to you." I gushed as he began to strum his guitar and sing. His voice was deep and rich like chocolate, and it went like this.

'The rooster on the roof,

Is calling out to you...

Coo coo doo coo coo,

Crying out for you...'

I laughed out loud. He stopped and gave me a serious look.

"Why are you laughing?" he teased, "We met on the roof next to that big rooster statue, didn't we?" I made a gesture that signalled that my lips were sealed, and he continued to sing.

'Every night I go to sleep,

Waiting for the dawn,

Hoping to see your face

In that familiar place.'

'The rooster on the roof...'

When he stopped, he said, "Well, it's still a work in progress. Do you like it?"

"Yes", I blushed, trying to gauge the implications of that song and whether it meant that he liked me too. I must have been quiet for a moment for he quickly changed the topic. All the while we were there, he alternated between conversation and songs. But these were other songs, safe songs. We ended our vigil in a couple of hours. When we pulled out the traps, there were five crabs in all. He skillfully tipped them into the bucket which was a re-used paint bucket with a lid. He shut the lid down tight so that the little creatures could not escape.

"Would you like to take these?" he offered, "Or is it too small a catch?"

"Yes, you better take it to your grandmother," I suggested while we walked home.

At the end of our morning together, I could not be certain of how he felt about me, not with the way he had deflected after that first song. We had exactly six more days together. I was set to leave the following Saturday and he'd told me that he would be leaving for Bombay soon after. It pained me to think that we were reaching the end of our time together. Perhaps it was better if things were left unsaid.

The days just flew past me and in the blink of an eye, it was Saturday. My father was to pick me up in the evening. I was all packed and set to go. Noah and I had spent time together every day. But on that Saturday morning, he wasn't on the roof. I called their landline, but Mrs. Monteiro told me that he wasn't at home. She had no idea where he'd gone or when he would return. Noah finally showed up at the house in the evening.

"Where were you?" I cried, "My dad will be here at any moment now."

"Sorry", he said smiling his contemplative smile, "I lost track of time."

We were both in the lower verandah of Avozinha's house. He came and sat down beside me, a few inches apart. We made small talk to pass the time and all the while my heart was breaking. I wondered whether he had the slightest inkling of how I felt. My time was up. My father arrived. He was in a rush as usual. I looked at Noah for the last time. I drank him in with my eyes and walked away. There were no cell phone numbers or email addresses to exchange back then, just landline numbers and postal addresses. I wondered whether I would ever see him again. And just like that, the most beautiful summer of my life ended.

Back home and in the days that followed, I was very lovesick. Noah had left for Bombay almost immediately after I left Siolim, without so much as a phone call. Then the board results were declared, and I was caught up in the frenzy of the admission process. At the end of it, I had gotten into the electronics engineering program at an engineering college in Goa. My parents were ecstatic, but I was rather indifferent. I entered engineering college with a lousy attitude.

I missed Noah terribly. His removal from my life had created a void that I was desperate to fill with anything or for that matter, anyone. And that is why I got into a relationship with a fourth-year senior in college, on the rebound. It was a terrible lapse of judgement on my part. I soon discovered that this boy was jealous and possessive. I broke it off with him within a couple of months. But it seems like he carried a torch for me for months thereafter and stalked me for the rest of the academic year. I was scared and shaken. It was only when the year ended and he passed out of college, that I finally had some peace. I just managed to scrape by in my first year. I chided myself for being so reckless and foolish. That torturous relationship with my senior had cured me of any romantic notions. I had a lot to prove to myself and my family. And so, from my second year onwards, I worked relentlessly without distraction. The thought of Noah did cross my mind now and then. I did not have a single souvenir of him, not even a photograph. Therefore, my time with him had become just a precious memory that I would cherish forever.

By the end of my second academic year in engineering, I had risen to the top of the class. I strove hard to maintain that position for the rest of my time there through sheer determination and grit. I had come to enjoy my specialization. In my third year, I was among the first in my batch to get placed in a good company. That year marked the onset of a terrible recession. But we were lucky to make a narrow escape. My job was secure. I joined my new firm in Bangalore soon after graduation. It was my first time away from home. I was discovering my independence and enjoying it. I visited home several times a year – on long weekends, Christmas, and other special family occasions.

Unbeknownst to me, Noah's star had begun to steadily rise in the music industry at around the same time when I had just started my career. Over the first few initial years, he contributed to the musical scores of movies and even put out an obscure album. The World

Wide Web had opened its doors to us by that point in time and I had thus discovered his music. I had taken to following his career closely and while his first album had not been of much consequence, his second had made waves on the national scene. He had garnered a steady fan base In India and more so in his home state of Goa.

However, his first album had a special place in my heart, for in it was a little rustic tune entitled *Rooster on the Roof*. It was the souvenir that I had always yearned for, and it was far more precious than a photograph. It was our song! He had recorded it in an acoustic arrangement with a guitar and local instruments like the ghumot.

When I first heard it, I laughed out loud and clapped my hands in delight. That sweet warm melody stirred up memories and emotions and warmed up my heart after what seemed like a very long time. I felt wonderful whenever I heard it. I wondered what it would be like to meet Noah now, years after our delightful summer together. But I lacked the nerve to pursue the matter. I seemed to have lost my appetite for romance and was committed to my career. I had even been on a couple of international assignments and had spent some time in Europe and the US.

Six years after graduating from engineering college, at the age of twenty-seven, I was a project manager, perhaps one of the youngest in the company. That's what absolute dedication to the job and the absence of social life will get you. My parents had begun to desperately nag me about marriage. They kept on inquiring whether

I had a secret boyfriend stashed away somewhere. I think they sincerely hoped that I did if it would get me a step closer to settling down and starting a family. The fact was that I simply did not have the time or the inclination for a boyfriend. I met several of the 'good boys' that my parents lined up for me. But things never clicked. My parents grew more and more disheartened with every proposal that I rejected. I was glad not to be living at home.

Then, one day, I heard from Rosie that Mrs. Monteiro, Noah's grandmother had passed away. I remembered how fond of her Noah was. I felt an unexpected urge to meet him, to console him, to hug him and reconnect after all this time. I flew down to Goa for the funeral. I felt the type of heady anticipation and nervousness that I had not allowed myself to feel in a long time. I had only told Rosie about my trip home and had made her promise not to tell my parents about it or the reason behind it. I wasn't in the mood for another set-up. I planned to go straight to Siolim church from the airport and after that, well, I would see how to deal with things.

The once-familiar church stood unfazed by time. I paid for the taxi to wait for me and left my small carry-on in the car. There were so many people! I hadn't expected such a huge crowd. Was it because of Mrs. Monteiro or because of her famous grandson? I wondered. Inside the church, it was standing room only and I tried my best to make my way as far inside as possible. But despite my best efforts, I was restricted to the back of the church. I tiptoed to get a better view, but it was just not possible. I could not focus on the service at all. I silently offered a prayer for Mrs. Monteiro, with a note of apology attached to it.

Then towards the end of the service, right when the crowded church was in its most silent and solemn moment, my phone rang loudly. I had set my ringtone to *Rooster on the roof* ages ago and now it reverberated through the large church. Several of the people surrounding me turned to give me disapproving looks. I was fumbling to find the phone in my large bag while it haplessly played, *'the rooster on the roof, is calling out to you, coo coo doo coo coo..'* I had no choice but to turn and flee outside of the church to stop it from disturbing the congregation any further. Once I was safely outside and managed to find the darned thing and switch it off, I realized that all my efforts to make headway inside the church had been nullified. I sighed in defeat and embarrassment.

I decided to remain outside of the church for the rest of the service. Perhaps I would have a better chance of getting closer to the family at the burial service in the cemetery. But it was not to be. There appeared to be a lot of people with a thought process similar to mine and I was left standing out again. I thought that I would at least get to meet the family in the condolence queue. People were already queuing up and I joined them hastily. Anticipation gripped me again. I would finally get to see if not meet Noah again. The line took forever, but when I got to the family, I could not find Noah anywhere. It was just an elderly couple who had to have been his parents, along with other assorted relatives. I was crushed. After dutifully offering my sympathies to the bereaved family, I wandered off to the church grounds. 'What happened?' I wondered, there was no way that Noah would miss his grandmother's funeral, would he?

I walked back into the church and wearily sat down in the pews at the back of the church. I let out a deep sigh to let out all my pent-up anticipation. I shook my head and chided myself over my foolishness. What had I expected? A grand sentimental reunion? Only close family friends were invited over to the deceased's residence for refreshments after the service. I was trying to figure out whether I was indeed that audacious when I felt a hand on my shoulder and looked up startled. It was Noah! He stood before me finally in the flesh and I had to give my tired brain a moment to register his presence. He had not changed at all, even his hairstyle was the same. The moment the image had sunk in, my heart began to sprint.

"Hi!" I gasped and nervously stood up to meet him. He was smiling at me. I was trying to remember which type of smile it was. I shook my silliness off.

"I am sorry about your grandmother, Noah", I said and held out my hand for a handshake. He took it and pulled me into an embrace. I felt all of the walls that I had built so painstakingly over the years crumble and hugged him back with all my might. He felt warm and smelt wonderful. When we drew apart, I was sorry to let him go.

"I knew that it had to be you", he laughed nervously. "That ringtone", he explained, "that song was not very well known at all."

I was staring at him unabashedly. "Where were you?" I cried.

"Oh, my grandpa's in a wheelchair. I had to stay back here with him." He explained and then he must have realized that my question had a much deeper connotation.

"Well, I am here now", he said and took both my hands into his, "and I am not going anywhere."

Then, he smiled at me: the dazzling happy smile that I remembered well. He pulled me into an embrace again. He felt warm, he smelt wonderful. He felt like home.

Glossary

Aiee baba – mother and father

Assado – roast meat dish

Athi sundar – very beautiful

Avarenta – miser (female)

Avozinha – grandmother

Bai – term of endearment (female)

Baba – term of endearment (male)

Bhatkar – landlord/ landowner (male)

Bhatkaan, bhatkanni – landlady/ landowner (female)

Cafreal – green gravy dish usually made with chicken

Caldo verde – creamy soup made of spinach and potato

Croquette – bite-sized cutlet

Dharvantto – back door, door of a backyard enclosed within a compound

Doce – sweet cake made of coconut or gram flour

El Caminho – type of bus used in the past

Ghumot – drum made of an earthen pot with leather stretched across its mouth

Kakonn – crisp bread in the shape of a large bangle

Katreacho pao – bow-shaped bread

Khoitho – heavy knife-like cutting tool

Licieu – secondary school in Portuguese regime

Mai – mother

Malcriado – Portuguese word for uncivilized

Mankurad – a delicious variety of mango found in Goa

Mattao – flat, roofed tent like structure

Munkar – tenant

Namaste – Indian way of greeting with folded hands

Paan-tobacco wrapped in beetle nut leaf used for chewing

Padvigar – vicar

Paltadi – the other side (of the river)

Pao – bread

Pensao – curse

Pescadora – fisherwoman

Pescador – fisherman

Poie – whole wheat bread

Podder – man who delivers bread

Pulao – flavoured rice dish

Recheado – a red masala made of vinegar, dried red chilies and spices, used to fry fish and seafood.

Resois – bite-sized snack with a filling of cheese etc.

Rozangno – internal garden contained within a large house

Sala – large Hall

Saurakh – curry made without fish or seafood, to be eaten with rice.

Seradura – rich dessert made of cream

Sopo – seat made of stone and cement

Tawa – flat pan

Tendli bhaji – vegetable dish made with gerkin-like fruit

Tulas – decorative planter for the holy basil plant which is considered sacred

Tika – mark made on the forehead by coloured powder/ liquid

Undo – hard-crusted bread

Vokhol – bride

Voiz – doctor

Xec xec – aromatic, flavourful gravy

Xacuti – coconut gravy dish made with some form of protein